ELIZABETH'S STORY

It seemed the ██████████ me
broke off and ████████████ thing.
It was so ██████████ ll
of me flowed back together again,
and I almost cried out. They
hanged witches! I was not a witch!
I am not a witch!

SALEM WITCH

ELIZABETH'S STORY

READ ELIZABETH FIRST THEN READ GEORGE

KINGFISHER
a Houghton Mifflin Company imprint
222 Berkeley Street
Boston, Massachusetts 02116
www.houghtonmifflinbooks.com

First published in 2006
2 4 6 8 10 9 7 5 3 1
1TR/0606/THOM/SGCH/80GSMSTORA/C

LIBRARY OF CONGRESS CATALOGING-IN-PUBLICATION DATA
has been applied for.

ISBN-13: 978-07534-5991-1
ISBN-10: 0-7534-5991-4

Printed in India

... E STORY

SALEM
WITCH

——— ✦ ———

ELIZABETH'S STORY

PATRICIA HERMES

KINGFISHER
BOSTON

Read Elizabeth's story first, then flip over
and read George's side of the story!

Author's note:

While this is a work of fiction and the characters of
Elizabeth and George are not based on real people,
much of the dialogue was taken from actual
transcripts of the Salem witchcraft trials, as well
as notes recorded by witnesses at the time.

Chapter One

"'Tis madness, it is, this talk of witches and devils. If it is devils you want, look to those girls, Betty and Abigail and Ann and the others. Since when have childish bad manners and behavior come to be the doings of witches?" I have heard Papa say that, or something like that, at least 100 times this winter. Each time, Mama nods in agreement and adds her own comments, as Mama is as thoughtful and well-read as Papa. They have both studied the works of Increase Mather, who has written about witchcraft, and Papa especially has a lot to say about it—mostly that it is pure foolishness. Yet here in Salem Village, there are few people who think the same as Mama and Papa.

The girls who started this talk of witches are Betty and Abigail—the daughter and niece of the minister, Reverend Parris. They have begun to have fits, and Dr. William Griggs says that it is no natural disease that afflicts them. It is, he says, witchcraft. Folk say that if a witch can enter such a holy place as the minister's house, it means that the devil is in our town. I do not believe it at all, and I agree with Papa and Mama that it is nonsense. I know those girls, and I have known them to be mean and wicked long before they began talking about witches. My cousin

Ann Putnam admitted to me at a family supper not long ago that she and Betty and Abigail had been playing with magic. They learned it from Tituba, the slave woman, when no grown people were around. Ann made me promise to keep it a secret, since playing with magic is forbidden here in Salem Village. But this talk of witchcraft has gone far beyond magic play. They are now clearly up to something evil.

Papa has warned us—Mama and me—to be careful about speaking these thoughts out loud, however. In such a time as this, Papa says, it is best to use caution. We must even be careful in our own household, since it is rumored that our maid, Mary Warren, is accusing others of witchcraft. Mama is determined to dismiss Mary soon.

So I do not speak out much. I am careful. But I am also angry.

I was thinking about these things as I crossed the field to the house of Goodwife Rebecca Nurse with some soup and bread that Mama had made for her. Goody Nurse has been sick, and Mama has taught me that those of us who have plenty should help those who are less fortunate. The February ground was hard and frozen beneath my feet, and sleet peppered my face. My head was bent down against the sleet, and when I looked up, I saw that two others were on the path ahead of me. George! George Corwin, my dear friend. He is the son of a friend of Papa's, and though he is a boy, we have been best friends for a very long time. He is also exceedingly handsome. In misty, wet weather, his dark hair sticks to his face, and he has long, thick eyelashes that any girl would envy. The other person ahead was my cousin Ann—the leader of those wicked girls.

"George!" I called out. "George Corwin."

George turned, smiling, then hurried to my side—or hurried as much as he could. George was injured by a kick from a horse some years ago, and he walks with a ferocious limp. "What are you doing out in this dreadful weather?" he asked when he had reached my side.

I nodded at the basket in my hands and smiled at him. "Some foodstuffs for Goody Nurse. She is feeling unwell. And what are you doing so far from the town?"

"I am here with Papa," George answered. "He sent me to the village to fetch some tobacco twists for him."

"Look, George!" I said. "Do you see what I see? Is that Ann Putnam up ahead?"

George looked, then nodded grimly. "It seems so." He paused and touched my arm gently. "Elizabeth, my papa is one of the judges who will examine Ann and the other girls tomorrow. That is why we are here in the village."

"Examine them?" I frowned at him.

"Yes. The girls and Tituba, the Parris' slave."

"I do not understand," I said. "Examine them for what?"

"Did you not hear? In court on the morrow, the girls will name the ones who bewitch them."

"Oh, that!" I cried. "Those girls are fakes, you know that. All this business of falling down in fits and saying that witches have pinched them is pure foolishness."

"You do not believe it?" he asked.

"No!" I said. "I do not. Do you?"

George frowned, but he did not answer.

"George?" I said.

He still did not reply.

I knew that I was being bold, foolish too, perhaps. I know George; I trust him. Since we were little ones, we have been the greatest of friends. But Papa's caution whispered in my ears not to speak about my feelings out loud. Still, I was too angry to pay much heed to Papa's words.

"You know that it is nonsense, George," I said. "You know that."

George pinched his lips together. "I do not know that, Elizabeth," he said. "Dr. Griggs says that it is no

8

physical illness that has overtaken Betty and Abigail. Those girls have fits and terrors most every day now. And . . ." Here George leaned in closer to me and spoke more softly. "Papa even says that Betty has begun hiding and racing around the room and crying out. She says that she is being pinched and tormented by Tituba and other witches."

"Tormented by witches? Perhaps by their own consciences, if one of them should have a conscience," I replied. "Betty is an evil little girl. I have seen her poke her sister with a pin from her clothing—and her sister is only a little one!"

"Truly? You saw that?" George asked.

I nodded. "A long time ago—months ago—before all this witchcraft talk began. And she did it in the meetinghouse too."

"Perhaps, Elizabeth," George said. "Yet Papa must question them. He has been asked to by Ann's parents."

I shook my head and did not answer. Sometimes, I am ashamed to be a Putnam myself, though my papa is not at all like his brother Thomas, Ann's papa.

"Have you heard who is accused?" George asked.

"I have heard rumors," I said. "Sarah Good and Sarah Osborne. And that is only because they are troublesome women."

"They are indeed troublesome," George answered.

"But that does not make them witches!" I

answered. "And if they are named and found guilty, then what?"

George shivered. "Let us hurry on," he said. "The rain is beginning to freeze."

"It is already frozen," I said. "What will happen to them? What will your papa do?"

George shrugged. "Perhaps . . . perhaps he will simply warn them."

"Or hang them!" I said. "I know. There is no need to hide it. Poor Mary Glover was hanged in Boston four years ago. Papa told me, and she was not a witch at all. She was just a plain, simple Irishwoman who had no education and no family and no one to speak up for her."

George did not look at me. "I do not believe that hangings will occur," he said.

"I will not allow it to occur!" I said. And how I could think that, I had no idea. But I am too impulsive in my speech, as Mama often tells me, and never more so than at that minute. Before I could help myself, I heard myself calling out, "Ann! Ann?"

George took my arm. "Do not do this!" he said softly. "She will only cause trouble. You know that. I truly believe the witches . . ."

I shook him off. "There are no witches!" I said angrily. "Ann Putnam!" I called again.

Ann turned to me. She had been hurrying, her cloak drawn tightly around her, the hood pulled down to protect her face from the sleet that was falling hard now. She looked up at me as I drew closer. "What do you want of me?" she asked, her voice sounding tight and haughty.

For a moment, I did not answer. What did I want with her? For her to tell me that she had been pretending? Did I really believe that she would tell me what she had not told anyone else? Or did I just want her to tell me who she would name so that I could warn them? But what good would that do? Sarah Good and Sarah Osborne had probably already heard and dismissed it as nonsense, laughing off such accusations. Besides, Sarah Good was a vagrant, sometimes living in barns and fields with her children, begging at back doors. Silly accusations from silly girls would be the least of her worries. Is that why Ann and her friends had focused on them, because they were easy targets?

Yet, looking at Ann, I could feel my heart thudding hard against my ribs. There was something fearful about her face. She was only 12 years old—my age—but there was a meanness in her face that unsettled me.

"What do you want with me, Elizabeth?" she asked. "And what are you doing going around with

George?" She gave a harsh look at George, who only grinned back at her.

"Why, we were holding hands as we walked, Miss Ann," he said. "Could you not see that for yourself?"

I giggled, because both my hands were clearly in use carrying Mama's basket of cakes and soup and bread.

"I was not with George," I retorted. "I have just met him as I have met you. And in this basket are foodstuffs for Goody Nurse. She is unwell."

"Unwell?" Ann said, blinking at me, the ice coating her thin lashes. "Perhaps she is unwell because there is evil within her."

"Goody Nurse?" I said, laughing. "Goody Nurse is far better than you will ever be."

Ann smiled, that mean, tight smile of hers, making her look much older than her years. Suddenly, she looked so much like her mama that I thought again of what my parents had suspected for a long time—that her own mama was behind some of these accusations of witchcraft.

"Do not even think of accusing Goody Nurse!" I said, and I was angry at myself, because my voice was trembling.

"Her spectral form tormented me last night. She pinched me."

"Then you deserved it!" I said.

"Elizabeth does not mean that!" George said, stepping forward so that he was between me and Ann. "She is simply troubled by all the talk of witches. We are all troubled."

"I do mean it!" I said. I pushed him aside so that I was face-to-face with Ann. "Ann!" I said. "We are cousins. Tell me. Why are you doing this?"

"I do nothing!" Ann said. "The specters do it."

"Ann," I said, "listen. You spoke about magic to me not long ago, not witchcraft. You spoke about games."

For a moment, Ann looked anxious. She slid a look at George. "I never said magic," she muttered.

"You did! You said that it was a game."

"Perhaps. Long ago," she retorted. "But now I know better. Tituba is a witch. She baked a witch cake and fed it to the dog."

I would have laughed. I wanted to laugh. I wanted to ask if the dog was now bewitched. But I was so unnerved by the look of evil on Ann's face, that for a moment, I could not speak.

"I would not meddle if I was you," Ann said. "Even children can be witches."

"Is that a threat?" I asked. Again, my voice trembled. But it was more with anger than with fear.

"The truth, that is all," Ann said. "You know, do you not, that Dorcas Good is a witch?"

"Dorcas Good?" I asked. "Dorcas? That little child?"

13

"So I said," replied Ann.

"She is no more a witch than am I! She is four years old! Or perhaps three."

"Four," replied Ann calmly.

"Elizabeth," George said, taking my arm. "Please. Shall we finish our walk?"

"I would not go with her to Rebecca Nurse's home," Ann said to George. "She may not be as sick as she pretends. Rebecca Nurse was out last night, riding on her stick."

"With Dorcas Good," I said. "Do not forget the four year old. Did Dorcas have a smaller stick than the others?"

"Little fingers can pinch as well as larger fingers," Ann said.

I set down my basket. "But larger fingers are stronger," I said.

And then I did what I knew was wrong, something that was against all of God's rules. Mama's rules too. I took Ann's hand gently in both of mine as though I was about to plead with her. And then, with great care, I pinched the skin on the back of her hand—that slight, tight skin where I knew that it would hurt the most.

She made a small, squealing sound, then yanked her hand away and held it against her. "You will regret that!" she said, almost spitting the words.

"Perhaps," I said. "But you can know that I did it.

Me. Not my specter. Me. And I have a witness here to prove it."

I picked up my basket. "Come, George," I said. "Goodwife Nurse is waiting."

Chapter Two

So that is how it all began—for me, that is. Those girls had been at it for some time. But now I had set myself against them, and I feared for what I had done. Still, what was done was done, and as I walked on to Goodwife Nurse's home with George by my side, my heart gradually became a bit calmer.

"You were brave to say what you said, Elizabeth," George said softly. "But you must be careful. Those girls have power."

"I was foolish to say what I said," I answered. "I know that. Nevertheless, I spoke the truth."

"How do we know what the truth is?" asked George.

I turned to him. "Tell me," I said. "Do you believe in witches?"

"I believe in the devil," he answered. "The devil can tempt people."

"Tempt them into what?"

"To come to his side. To sign his book."

"And what would that do?" I asked.

George moved closer to me then. "Elizabeth," he said softly. "I almost drowned a few days ago. I had been sketching in the woods. It was dark, and I was coming home along the path through the woods and over the creek. My horse, Hector, reared up and whinnied, as though he had seen something dreadful.

I was tossed off, and we both tumbled over and over, me and Hector both. He landed on top of me. I crashed through the frozen creek, almost breaking my neck, and lay there a while, half drowned, before I came to my senses."

"Oh, George!" I cried. "How dreadful. How . . ."

"Tituba knew about it. The very next morning, she told other folk what had happened. Yet no one had spoken about it outside my home. It happened at night. We live miles apart. How could she have known? My papa thinks that her specter—her spirit—left her body to come and frighten Hector. Maybe to kill me."

For a moment, I could not speak, thoughts were twirling around in my head. Up ahead, I could see Rebecca Nurse's home, I could see smoke rising from her chimney, and I focused on that, thinking about sitting there a while, warming ourselves. I simply could not believe that a specter could leave one's body and taunt and tease others. And I certainly could not believe that it could try to kill others.

"Do you believe that it was Tituba?" I asked.

"No," George answered. "No, I do not. I believe that it was a fox. I actually saw its tail as it scurried into the undergrowth, just before I fell."

I breathed a sigh of relief. George was not swept away with the nonsense that was going on. George is even more bookish than me. Having been injured at a young age, he is not able to be out, running around like other boys—though he rides incredibly well. But he also spends time studying. He reads the Bible, as I do, but he also reads many other books. It would be almost unbearable to think that he, my dear friend, could believe in such nonsense.

"But, Elizabeth," George went on. "Papa says that witches have familiars—animals and others who act for them, who take on their specters to harm others."

"Yes, I have heard that. But do you believe it?" I persisted. "That it was Tituba's specter in the fox?"

"No," he said, and he smiled at me—that sweet, sweet smile that he has—and for a moment, I felt my heart sing. He was not caught up in the madness! Not at all. He was still my friend—the same boy that I had known for years. But then he added, "No, I do not believe it. Not now. But I want to see and hear what happens at the questionings."

"That is fair," I said. Because I knew that once he saw and heard the foolishness, he would understand. "But you know, you will hear nonsense."

"Perhaps," he said, and again he smiled at me.

We were at Goodwife Nurse's home by then, and she opened the door for us, ushering us into her warm kitchen. She looked pale and was bent over, as though she was in pain. But she was clearly pleased to see us and made us sit in front of her fire.

"What a good, kind woman your dear mama is," she said, as we got ourselves settled. "How kind to send such good things to me. And you, to come out on such a day, dear Elizabeth. With your companion, George."

"I am happy to be here," I replied. "Though it is a fierce day out there."

Goodwife Nurse leaned her head close to mine, since she was hard of hearing. "What sort of day?" she asked.

"Fierce!" I said. "I said that it was a fierce day outside."

"It is," she said. "'Tis hard to even keep the fire from flickering, the way the wind blows down the chimney." She smiled at me. "It is said that witches have caused these terrible gales and storms these past two days."

I smiled back at her. I had heard that too, along with all the other talk.

"I also hear that there are terrible afflictions in the village," Goody Nurse went on. "Some girls have been afflicted with fits?"

"Yes," I replied. "That is what they say."

"I have not gone to visit them yet," she said. "Do you know, I once had fits myself when I was a girl. They pass, these things."

I wondered if this was the time to warn her, to tell her what Ann Putnam had said. But what good would

19

it do? Besides, I doubted that anyone would really believe that Rebecca Nurse could do evil, no matter what Ann and the others said. Still, just to be named would be a dreadful thing.

"And why are you in the village, George?" Goody Nurse asked, turning to George. "Is your father not in court in Boston?"

"No," George answered. "No, he is not."

Goody Nurse raised her eyebrows at George— a look that clearly asked a question. I could see that it disturbed George, because he fidgeted and looked away, examining the fire poker as though he had never seen such an implement in his life. I was sure then that Goody Nurse had some idea why George might be here in town. Even though she had not been out because of her illness, she had a son-in-law in the village who may have brought her the news.

"Is he holding court here?" Goody Nurse asked.

George straightened himself up and looked at her. "Yes. That is so. The Putnam family requested a hearing."

"And there will be accusations?"

George nodded.

"And who will the girls accuse?" asked Goody Nurse. "The vagrant, Sarah Good? That silly Tituba?"

George and I exchanged looks.

If Goody Nurse saw our look, she ignored it.

"Tituba is a foolish person," she went on. "I have heard that she baked a witch cake to cure Betty's illness."

"Ann said that also," I said. "They fed it to the dog."

Goody Nurse shook her head, and for a long while, she did not speak. Her brow became furrowed, and she stared into the fire, just as George was doing. After a while, she turned to me.

"Yes," she said at last. "I was told that Tituba took some of Betty's urine, mixed it with I-know-not-what, and fed it to the dog. Tituba seems to believe that it will take the evil out of Betty or any afflicted person. And perhaps point to who is bewitching her."

"Did the dog become bewitched?" I asked. And I have no idea why that question popped out of me as it did. If I could wonder, did I not believe in witches?

Goody Nurse smiled. "Nobody is bewitched, Elizabeth, dear. You know that." She turned to George. "And I hope that your papa knows that too."

George looked up, his eyes worried. "Papa gave me Increase Mather's book to read. It is called *Remarkable Providences*, and it tells about witchcraft and supernatural events."

"And you believe all of that?" asked Goody Nurse.

"No," said George. "No, I do not. Even Increase Mather says that some things cannot be explained. But listen!" And here, George's voice got all strange and fearful sounding, and he leaned forward to us.

"I read how William Morse's house was bewitched. One night, there was a hog running wild in his house in Newberry, yet the doors had been locked, and there was no opening for the hog to come through. And so they prayed and prayed and called upon God . . ."

"And . . ." Goody Nurse interrupted, smiling, "and then, the hog ran out! But first, they had to open the door for it."

I bit back my laughter. How true!

"You see," Goody Nurse went on. "Prayer is good. Prayer is necessary. But one must open doors also."

But George was not finished yet. "Yes, but Increase Mather's son, Cotton Mather, has also written. He wrote . . ."

"Cotton Mather is even more of a fool than his father," Goody Nurse said.

Truly, I could have leaped up and thrown my arms around Goody Nurse's neck. What a joy! What a surprise. Perhaps it is, as Papa says, that even evil times can bring some good. I had had no idea that Goody Nurse was so wise, so thoughtful—and so well-read.

"Just because something is written," Goody Nurse went on, leaning toward George, "does not mean that it is true. There are many learned books in this world—and many rather stupid ones." She smiled at me. "And, I am afraid, stupid people, too. Now, may

I make a hot drink for you?"

I was longing for a hot drink, but I had already been gone too long, and Mama would be waiting for me to do my other chores for her.

"I must go," I said, standing up and pulling my now-warmed cloak around me. "Mama is waiting for me. But I thank you for your kindness."

George also got to his feet.

"And I thank you for your kindness," Goody Nurse said. "I will thank your mama myself when I am well again. Already, my stomach seems not to hurt so much. Kindness can be healing, can it not?"

I nodded.

Goodwife Nurse put a hand on my shoulder briefly. "Go," she said. "Godspeed."

"God bless," I said back.

"God bless," she said to George, though she did not put a hand on his shoulder.

"God bless," George answered, and we departed.

Once we were outside, I could feel my heart singing. This whole business could not be so bad. There were normal people—learned, healthy-minded people, like Mama and Papa and Goody Nurse, and maybe many others—who clearly did not believe. The witch trials, if that is what they were to be called, would be over in a day. And the evil girls would be shown for what they were—liars and fakes.

And I hoped—I really, really hoped—that no one, certainly not Goodwife Nurse, would be hurt before it was all over.

Chapter Three

The following morning, when the hearings were to start, I was bitterly disappointed when Papa forbade me to attend. The hearings were to be held at Ingersoll's Tavern, and Papa and the tavern keeper had had many grievances with each other—some of them disagreements about the witchcraft accusations.

"But, Papa!" I said. "I will not even speak to Samuel Ingersoll, nor to his wife, nor anyone! Please! You are always urging me to know what happens in our village and to take part. These are important affairs."

"True," Papa said, smiling.

"Then why will you not allow me to go? Just yesterday, you said how proud you are of me that I am not overcome by superstition like some of these silly women and girls. You say that all of the time."

Again, Papa smiled. "That is also true."

"Then?" I knew I was being bold, but I was so angry. "Then here is a chance to learn!"

"Daughter," Papa said, and he came and led me to a chair and handed me a book. "Spend this morning reading. I will report everything back to you. I will not leave out a single thing, I promise you. I have reasons for this decision."

Then he turned and left the room. I made a face at his back, but I knew that there was no sense in arguing. When he makes up his mind, there is no changing it. I looked down at the book and grimaced. It was another of Increase Mather's treatises that Papa wants me to know about—so that I can intelligently argue against it, he says.

As I read, I tried to pay attention, but my mind kept drifting, thinking about Papa and Mama, and even Samuel Ingersoll, and how my family is different from most people here in Salem Village. First, we are not Puritans but Quakers, though Mama and I often attend Reverend Parris' church here. Also, Papa is an important person. He owns a fleet of ships and has commerce in Salem Town, so he meets many different kinds of people with different kinds of ideas. He is also educated—a graduate of Harvard—and to him, there are few things that are more important than learning. Perhaps that, the love of learning, is the most important way that we are different from others in the village. Papa even says that some day girls might be able to attend Harvard. Imagine!

I sometimes wonder if Papa had had a son, if he would treat me differently. But I do not think so. I truly believe that Mama and Papa both prize book learning above almost everything else, whether it is a girl to be educated or a boy. It does make us different from most people here in the village.

I quickly became tired of my reading, and I sought out Mama in the kitchen. She could have gone to the hearing, but did not want to. She said that it was simply theater and that there was nothing to be learned. So, for that whole morning, I dithered. I did a bit of this and a bit of that, even getting in the way of Mary Warren, our maid, until Mama told me that if I did not settle down, she would put me to work with a needle and thread. Mama knows that is one of the toughest punishments I could have.

Then, around mid morning, Papa came home. The location of the hearing had been changed. Ingersoll's Tavern had become so crowded that the hearing was moved to the meetinghouse, where we gather on Sundays to hear God's words. Papa would now allow me to go with him!

Oh, I was so overjoyed when Papa took my arm, and together we walked the short quarter mile, a bit of bread and cheese tucked inside our cloaks in case the hearing went on for the entire day. On the way, Papa warned me to stay back a fair distance from the accused and accusers, in case that they became violent with each other. I agreed, though a small part of me—was this evil?—was thrilled by the thought of what I might see. Even now, I tried to walk sedately, but I found myself pulling on Papa's arm until he spoke sharply to me, and I slowed down.

The meetinghouse was so crowded that it seemed as if the entire town had turned out. Papa worked his way to the front of the room near the communion table that was to be used as the judge's bench, but I was forced to settle myself farther back, according to Papa's instructions. Though it was a bitter cold day, the room was warmed by the many bodies, and I realized that it was the first time I could remember that room being warm.

Across the room, I saw my good friend Susannah Bishop—my only friend, actually, besides George. Her family is more like my family than any other, even though they are Puritans. I knew from talking to Susannah that her family did not believe in this witch business any more than we did. I signaled to her with my eyes, and she slowly began moving along the wall, making her way through the crowd to where I stood. She lay a hand on my arm.

"Is this not thrilling?" I said to her. "Papa says that I must be here to learn!" I looked around me, then leaned in close and whispered. "But I do believe that it is quite thrilling too. You do not believe in this business, do you?"

"I?" Susannah whispered back. "Do not be silly. But I was so distracted that I broke a teapot this morning, then used salt instead of powder, and both the bread and cake were ruined!"

I smiled at her, and we both turned and watched as the judges settled in. There were two—Judge Corwin, George's father, and Judge Hathorne. I have not met Judge Hathorne before, though of course I know George's father well. They walked in proudly, their long cloaks flapping behind them, and there was something majestic and even frightening about them. I was very glad that it was not I who was being called upon to accuse—or to be accused!

They settled themselves on one side of the Lord's Table, their backs against the wall of the meetinghouse. On the other side of the Lord's Table stood the accused: Sarah Good, Sarah Osborne, and Tituba. Sarah Osborne and Tituba seemed dejected and frightened, their eyes downcast, their hands clenched tightly, as though they were trying to hide their trembling. Sarah Good, however, was clearly angry. She tossed her head and glared at those around her. Other folk were milling around here and there, and the meetinghouse was loud and chaotic. I looked around for George and saw him leaning against a wall not far from me, his eyes fixed on his father. I kept sending him looks, but he was so intent on watching his father that he did not notice me.

Judge Hathorne signaled for silence, then stood up to pray. Immediately, the room became quiet. The prayer was mercifully short—Puritans have a habit of making dreadfully long prayers—and when it was over, everyone sat down—everyone, that is, except for those of us crammed in the aisles.

George's father signaled for the accusers to be led in—Abigail and Betty, the niece and daughter of our minister, as well as Elizabeth Hubbard and my cousin Ann. They came in demurely, their eyes downcast, and stood in a row in front of the judges. There was an expectant air in the room, as if we were all holding our breath. I studied Ann, wondering what she was thinking. Did she realize that this was serious now, not a time for acting? She and the other girls remained silent.

"Look upon them!" someone from the crowd suddenly shouted out. "Look upon the witches!"

As one, the girls raised their heads. Slowly, they turned to face the accused.

Suddenly, Abigail's arms flew high up over her head as though they had been seized by a ferocious force. Then, just as violently, her arms were twisted down and flung behind her back. She grimaced and writhed, tossing to and fro, as though she was being pulled apart by wild forces, something unseen and evil. Betty gnashed her teeth and flailed her arms, and Elizabeth's head began twisting around and around in almost impossible circles. Then, Elizabeth began crying out, a kind of babble, shouting out words that were impossible to decipher, as though she spoke a language foreign to the rest of us.

I felt fear leap like a flame into my chest and my throat. Was this real? Were they possessed? No! I did not believe that. I could not believe that.

Ann, twisted in similar contortions, began to cry out. "Be gone! Oh, be gone from me. Why do you torment me so? Why do you do these things? You pinch, you bite! Leave me, leave me!"

At that, it seemed as though she was lifted into the air and then flung down, her head smashing against the floor with a horrific thud. The sound made the entire meetinghouse go silent. Even the other girls became silent, no longer writhing and tossing themselves around.

For several long moments, Ann lay apparently senseless as her mama hurried to her side and bent down to her.

In the sudden silence, Judge Hathorne spoke. "Who torments you so?" he asked, his voice booming.

There was no answer. Ann lay as still as one who was dead. Was she dead? Had the witches killed her?

I slid a look at Susannah. She met my eyes, her own wide-open with fear, and we gripped each other's hands tightly.

After a moment, Ann began to stir, and I felt my breath rush out of me, as though unconsciously I had been holding it in. Ann's mama helped her slowly onto her feet.

"Who torments you so?" Judge Hathorne asked again, his voice softer now, seeming not to want to frighten Ann and make her burst into convulsions again.

Ann breathed deeply. "The witches," she whispered, leaning into her mama. Limp, she held out her arm toward the suspects. "Them. The witches!"

"Why do they torment you so?" Judge Hathorne asked. "Tell us."

Ann began trembling again, so violently that it seemed as if her body could not contain herself. She shook, her jaw tightened, and her eyes rolled as wildly as a frightened mare. Her mama held her tightly around the waist, and it took a few more long moments before Ann recovered enough to speak.

"The devil!" she whispered into the silence. "We were approached by the devil. He ordered us to sign his book. We said nay. Nay, we would not. He said he would send his witches to torment us."

"His witches," Judge Corwin repeated. "Who are his witches?"

Ann, still clinging to her mama, turned toward the accused. "There they stand!" she said.

Instantly, her body was seized, twitching and shivering, and her eyes rolled back into her head. At that very moment, the other girls also burst into convulsions, twisting and gasping for breath, backs bent, arms flung around them, their necks curved and twisted into almost unbelievable contortions.

I have seen children with fever and delirium. It is a terrifying thing. But this was even more horrible— perhaps because it was a performance? Or was it because it was the work of the devil? I did not believe that, did not! Still . . . I had to look away.

And in looking away, I looked around me, all around the meetinghouse. Every eye was fixed on the girls. And, at least to my way of seeing, there was not a nonbeliever in the room.

Chapter Four

After a short break for the noon meal, the afternoon questioning began. It was not with the girls, although they remained in the courtroom, but with those who were accused of witchcraft. On this day, the accused were Sarah Good, the vagrant woman who, with her family, sometimes lived in the woods or empty barns, Sarah Osborne, who had a reputation for being troublesome, though she had surely never disturbed my family, and Tituba, the dark-skinned slave woman who was said to have baked the witch cake.

I knew from my papa that in court an accused person was not permitted to stand silent. She must reply, no matter how many times she was asked a question, and sometimes—as I learned that afternoon—she was asked the same question again and again. She was not permitted to sit, either. Sometimes, she was even ordered to stand with her arms outstretched for the entire time. She did not have anyone to speak for her, such as an attorney. She was totally alone in front of the judges and those who had accused her.

My friend Susannah had returned home at the noon break, and as the afternoon questioning began, George made his way to my side. Even though his father was one of the judges, I felt happy having him by my side—my oldest, dearest friend. His papa took the lead for the afternoon, beginning with Sarah Good.

And the scenes that began to unfold were so horrific that, though I am ashamed to admit it, I actually felt faint. I did not dare leave, though, because I could not let Papa know how weak in spirit I was. Also, with the hysteria, who knew what might happen—if I was seen leaving, could I also be accused? Though I could not close my ears to the wailing and accusations, I was able to bend my head and close my eyes. Perhaps I should have remained at home.

It was only when the room burst into an uproar, with people shouting and crying out for the accused to be hanged, that I suddenly felt courage—and anger—flow back into me. I straightened myself up and looked steadfastly at the judges. If I, a firm disbeliever in this foolishness, had no courage, who would? And so I listened and watched—and took notes in my head.

What was I witnessing, I asked myself.

Panic? Lies? Surely, there were no such things as witches—especially witches that could cause these girls to be tormented like this? Was it not theater? But then . . . what was happening? And more than that— why? My head was dreadfully muddled by the time Judge Hathorne began questioning Tituba.

"Who is hurting the girls?" Judge Hathorne asked.

"The devil, for aught I know," Tituba replied.

"You know that?"

Tituba nodded. "I have seen him."

I gasped. And I truly believe that so too did everyone else in the meetinghouse. To actually have seen the devil was what everyone feared—or perhaps hoped for.

"You have seen the devil?"

"I have seen the devil," Tituba replied.

"How doth the devil appear when he hurts them?" Judge Hathorne asked.

Tituba was silent for a moment, and when she did finally reply, she spoke slowly, haltingly, for she is an Indian woman. "Like a man, I think," she said. "Oné day, I being in the lean-to chamber, I saw a thing like a man. It told me: serve him. And I told him no, I would not do such a thing. And then he say he will kill the children, Betty and Abigail. And if I do not serve him, me also."

"A man?" Judge Hathorne repeated. "The devil appeared like a man?"

"Yes, sometimes like a man. This was when the children was first hurt. But sometimes now, he comes like a hog."

I looked at George, and he at me, and I know what we were both thinking—about the hog who ran wild in Increase Mather's tales.

"A hog or a black dog or a red cat," Tituba went on. "And I remember this, too. I remember the great black dog. He say: serve me. And I tell him I am afraid. And then I say: I will not. And then he changes, and he looks like a man. And then the dog and the red cat come."

"Do you get the cat or the dog to hurt those children for you? Tell us, how is it done?"

Again, Tituba was silent for a while. "The man sends the cats to me and bids me use them to pinch the children," she said finally. "And then four women come and hurt the girls."

"Women?" Judge Hathorne asked. "And who are those four women?"

"I know two. Two I do not know. But I know Sarah Good. And Sarah Osborne."

Once again, the meetinghouse burst into an uproar. Men shouted out, and some even cursed, while others rushed forward, as though they would attack all the women. Judge Corwin ordered all three women to be taken away and held in jail. And in the uproar, court was adjourned for the day.

As I made my way out of the meetinghouse with George, my heart was pounding furiously. I could not wait to converse with my papa. What had I just witnessed? What was truth? What was theater?

"George," I whispered. "Do you believe that the devil did those things?"

George did not answer.

"George?" I said again.

He slipped his arm through mine. "We have heard such terrible things. I am afraid, Elizabeth."

I nodded. I was afraid too. But did I fear the same things that George feared? I did not believe what I had heard. But how could I account for what I had seen this morning?

We had reached the back of the meetinghouse by then, and I said farewell to him and went outside to look for Papa. I found him in conversation with Reverend Parris, Betty's papa. I wanted to hear what was being said, but I knew that it was not appropriate for me to interfere. However, I thought that it was not inappropriate to eavesdrop a bit. So I sidled up close, but when Papa sent me a warning look, I backed up a bit.

Why is it, I wondered, that I was not allowed to listen—especially when Papa had purposely invited me to accompany him to learn about all of this? But I made myself be patient and did so by playing a game inside of my head. As people passed by, I tried to guess what they were thinking by studying their faces, and especially their eyes. I thought that many were worried. But many seemed excited, too. And I remembered how thrilled I had felt this morning. It seemed now that had been a very long time ago.

After a while, Papa came to me, and we started home in the gathering dusk. I held on tightly to his arm.

"Papa?" I said. "Papa, what think you?"

Papa pressed my arm more closely to his own. "It was frightening," he said. "Was it not?"

"Very, Papa," I answered.

"Perhaps I should not have allowed you to come."

"Oh, no, Papa!" I cried out. "I had to come. You know that. I have to know. But what think you?"

Papa was silent for a while. And then he said, "You wonder if indeed there are witches?"

I was ashamed. But I had to answer with the truth. "Yes, Papa. I wonder."

"I can understand why you would," Papa said. "There was some wonderful acting up there today."

"Yes, Papa, the girls. But Tituba? She admitted."

"Tituba is a slave," Papa replied. "Perhaps she says what she has been told to say. Perhaps it is just magic tricks that she has done. Even those who worship in Reverend Parris' church have been known to practice magic tricks. You know that."

"Yes, but you always say that it is nonsense."

"Right," Papa said. "And so it is. Remember last year when you told me that some of you girls were looking into a glass with an egg—is that what it was? To see who your future husband would be?"

I giggled. We had all warned each other never to

speak about it. But I had told Papa, the way I tell him most everything, especially things that worry me.

"Yes, Papa, but that was nonsense, yes?"

"Yes," Papa answered. "So it was, and so this is. It is not witchcraft. Remember that Tituba is owned by Reverend Parris. She is not free. Perhaps she was beaten to say what he wanted her to say."

"But why would he want her to say that?"

Papa sighed. "I do not know, Elizabeth. There is the war with the Indians up in Maine, and that brings its own fears—especially since Tituba is an Indian. So, does Reverend Parris really believe in the work of the devil? Or is it evil of another kind going on here? You know that there are factions in this town, my very own brother and his family against the Porters against almost everyone else. And Reverend Parris—he is in league with the Putnams, some of them, anyway. He is an unhappy man."

"I have heard that the village people will not pay his salary," I said.

Papa nodded. "I delivered him some firewood myself this past night."

"You did, Papa? Why?" I asked, for I knew that Papa had a very dim view of Reverend Parris.

"You would have allowed him to freeze in his own house?" Papa said. He smiled down at me. "Though I do believe sometimes it would do him good."

40

"George believes in witches," I said. "I think that he does."

"George is his father's son," Papa said. "He will think what his papa thinks."

We walked on through the twilight, each of us quiet, thoughtful. I was wondering—if my papa believed in witches, would I believe too? Or would I not?

After a while, just as we approached Ingersoll's Tavern, we heard voices ahead, angry and frightened, and Papa's hand tightened on my arm. Through the mist, I could make out two men bending down low, peering at something beside the road.

"Good evening," Papa said, when we came alongside them.

They straightened up with a jerk and turned to us, and I recognized them as village folk, William Good and Alexander Osborne, the husbands of Sarah Good and Sarah Osborne, the women who had been accused. Both men had stood up in court that day and denounced their wives.

"They were there! Crouching right there!" William Good said, pointing to a place just off the path.

"And then they flew apart!" Alexander Osborne said.

"Who? What flew apart?" Papa asked.

"Them! The witches," William Good said. "All huddled together, looked like a beast. And when we came close to it . . . it . . ."

"It flew apart!" Alexander Osborne finished for him. "Turned into three of them. The beast turned into three witches."

"You know who them witches was, too," William Good said. "You was there. You heard them. You heard what they said."

"They are all locked up now," Papa said.

"Locked up, they may be. But their specters was here all right. Right here."

"Right here," said Alexander Osborne. "And we will not be safe until they be locked in chains. A jail will not hold 'em."

Both men were unsteady, shaking with fear, I thought. But then, as I stepped closer to William Good and caught a whiff of his breath, I realized that it was more like alcohol that was making them unsteady. And then I thought—was it alcohol that had caused them to cry out against their wives?

"Why not go on home, now?" Papa said gently. "I will walk a way with you to see that you get there safely."

"Ha!" Alexander Osborne said. "And who are you that you can protect us from the devil?"

"Not from the devil," Papa said smiling. "But I can help protect you from the ice beneath our feet." He took Alexander Osborne's arm with one hand, and, letting go of my arm, he reached out for William Good with the other, but William Good ducked away.

"It has begun to freeze again," Papa said. "Come along."

But William Good still held back, shivering and looking around him, as though he expected the witches to come back at any moment. "Nay, I seen them. I seen them," he said. "Right there, they were."

"Well, they are gone now. Come along," Papa said, reaching out again for William Good's arm. "My daughter here and I will see you safely home. It has been a horrid, long day."

"That, it has," William Good said, finally allowing Papa to take his arm. "And with more horror to come. Plenty more to come."

And that, I thought, was exactly, and sadly, the truth.

Chapter Five

One might have thought that the town would be calmer after this—the supposed witches locked up, and the girls silent. Mama was convinced that soon the accused women would be released with only a warning, and with the drama over, and the girls having had their share of attention, things would return to normal. Mama believed that this was all due to the girls wanting attention.

Papa, though, thought differently. He was convinced that more accusations were to come, since the two factions in town were still feuding. He felt certain that Ann was being spurred on by her mama and would soon accuse those with whom the families argued, even over such things as property lines. It worried me, because Papa is out in town more than Mama and me, and so he hears the rumors and concerns.

As for me, I alternated. One day, I was convinced that all was becoming calm. And the next day, I would hear something that worried me. One thing that worried me greatly was the condition of Sarah Good's little child, Dorcas. Sarah and her husband are vagrants, without any real home, and with her mama in jail, Dorcas was often seen wandering the streets, badly clothed against the cold, and begging at back doors.

Late one afternoon, around two weeks after her mama had been jailed, she appeared at our door. Mama and Papa, along with our servant girl, Mary Warren, had ridden into Salem Town for provisions. I was at home alone, when I heard a scratching at the door. When I opened it, I saw Dorcas standing there, a ragged cloak pulled around her.

For a moment, I was too startled to speak. And perhaps my look frightened her, because she suddenly turned and scurried away from me. She stopped back by the orchard.

"Dorcas?" I called. "Dorcas Good? What is it? Are you hungry?"

She did not answer.

"You do not need to be afraid," I called.

She did not reply, but she did not run farther, either. I could see her crouching in the mist, like a frightened rabbit.

I stepped away from the door and walked slowly across the frozen ground, holding out my hand to her, the way one might approach a wary animal. "It is just me," I said softly. "Come. If you are hungry, I will give you something. Are you hungry?"

She backed farther away, her eyes wide-open.

"I shall leave you be, Dorcas," I said. "I shall go back to my kitchen and leave the door open. Inside, on the table, is a warm apple tart. There is cheese. And, if you wish, I shall make you some hot broth."

She did not reply, but she nodded. She was shivering so hard that it was difficult not to reach out and pull her into my arms. I knew for certain, though, that she would fight me and flee if I did that. And so, with a calm that I did not feel, I turned and walked slowly back to the house.

At the door, I paused for a moment. The fire had begun to flicker in the hearth as the wind swirled in the kitchen. But I could not shut the door on that child. Instead, I heaped more wood upon the fire and poured some broth into the kettle.

Darkness had begun to fall, and I knew that Mama and Papa would return soon. I hoped that the noise of their cart would not frighten Dorcas away before she could get something to eat. Minutes passed slowly. I watched the clock on the mantle. After two or three minutes, the back door opened. I decided not to turn around yet, to allow Dorcas a moment to take in her surroundings. I waited another minute or so before I finally turned to see her standing just inside the door.

"The fire is hot," I said. "Will you come in and warm yourself?"

She nodded and took a few steps closer, but again, she stopped.

"It is all right," I said. "You warm yourself, and

I will prepare some food."

She scuttled her dirty little self close to the fire. I took the cheese from the larder and some thick bread that Mama had baked that day. I added some pieces of beef to the broth. I had to come close to Dorcas to do that, but she seemed so hungry, so fixed on the food, that she was less afraid. She simply watched me, her eyes wide and wary.

"Dorcas," I said, keeping my eyes fixed on the kettle. "Where do you sleep at night? Where is your papa?"

"Mama went away," she whispered.

"Yes," I said. "I know."

"My baby is gone."

I turned to her. "Your baby?"

She nodded. And then I remembered—Sarah Good had an infant, an infant daughter. Had they sent the baby to jail too? But, of course. If she was a suckling child, she would be with her mama.

"Where do you sleep?" I asked again.

Dorcas shrugged.

"Where is your papa?"

Again, she shrugged.

"Oh, Dorcas!" I said. And there must have been something in my voice that frightened her, because she looked toward the door.

"Do not be afraid," I said. I forced my voice to

become soft. "Here is your broth." I set a bowl on the table and poured the broth and some fat pieces of meat into it. I set out a spoon and the cheese. I moved slowly, not looking directly at her, though I peered at her from my lowered lids.

She approached the table. There, she took the bowl, but she left the spoon. She moved back to the fire and squatted on the floor, the bowl lifted up to her lips. She slurped thirstily, hungrily, devouring everything in the bowl and licking it out, like a small dog. When it was all gone, she lifted it toward me.

"Would you like more?" I said.

She nodded.

"Some cheese?" I asked.

Again, she nodded.

I went and poured more soup, then cut a thick slice of cheese. This time, I did not bother putting the bowl on the table. I simply brought it to her and set it and the entire cheese platter on the hearth next to her.

"Dorcas," I said softly, "can I take your cloak and dry it by the fire while you sup?"

She did not answer, simply shrugged the cloak off her shoulders and let it fall to the floor, while again she put her small face into the bowl. Under the cloak, her shoulders were alarmingly thin, her dress was tattered and filthy. It may have once had a color, but it was impossible to tell what it had been. I wondered then about some of my clothing that no longer fit. I have more dresses than most girls, and Mama often gave them to folk in need. But perhaps there were some that Mama had not given away that would fit Dorcas—or that we could cut down for her.

I lay her cloak on the chair by the fire, spread out so that it would get warm and dry. I saw that it, too, was so threadbare that I could not see how it could possibly keep the child warm. Surely, I could at least find her some thick, woolen undergarments?

"Dorcas?" I said. "Would you like something sweet? A tart?" She had finished the second bowl of soup in an alarmingly short time.

She nodded, her small body seeming to relax a little, but she was clearly still hungry. I worried about overfeeding her. Was it not harmful to eat too much after being hungry for a long time?

But I did not need to worry about that, because at that moment, she closed her eyes. She let herself slide down, slumping to the floor. She curled up on her side, raised her fist to her mouth, and began to suck on one finger noisily. In a moment, she was asleep.

I waited a little while so that I could be sure that she was sleeping soundly. Then, I took a warm woolen blanket that Mama keeps by the fire and spread it out over her. She murmured a bit and her finger slid out of her mouth, but she stuck it back in and began sucking noisily again.

I got up then, praying that Mama and Papa would return soon. Surely, we could do something for this child. Mama and Papa would not let her disappear into the freezing night to sleep in a barn.

Quietly, I tiptoed out of the room. I lit a candle, then crept up the stairs to my bedroom. We have a very large house—perhaps the largest and grandest house in the village. I have heard it said that it causes some envy among the village folk. I went through the things in my chest and found some woolen undergarments that were too small for me. I knew that they were large for Dorcas, but perhaps she could bunch them up. At least they would keep her warm.

At that moment, I heard the beat of the horses' hooves and the clacketty clack of the wagon wheels. Through the side window, I could see Mama and Mary dismount from the cart while Papa held the horse's head still. I hurried down the stairs, hoping to tell them to hush, so that they wold not startle the child.

But I did not need to worry. Dorcas was no longer sleeping. In fact, Dorcas was no longer there. She had grabbed her cloak and the entire hunk of cheese that I had set beside her, and she was gone into the night.

Chapter Six

On a Sunday in late March, something awful and awesome occurred, yet it was humorous, too—at least, at first. I was seated in the meetinghouse with Mama on one side and my friend Susannah and her mama on my other side. In the pew in front of us was Mama's friend Martha Corey, and in front of her was Abigail Williams. Abigail had made those nasty accusations in court, but for the past week or two, neither she nor any of the others had said more. I was ready to believe that the whole thing was settling down, though Papa still thought otherwise.

On this morning, Reverend Lawson was the guest preacher, but no sooner had he begun to preach than Abigail did something so amazing that I felt my heart leap into my throat.

"You!" she shouted, jumping to her feet and thrusting her hand toward the reverend. "You, reverend. Name your text."

Reverend Lawson looked down from the pulpit, seemingly stunned. For a long moment, he said nothing, his face going pale and looking stricken.

"Name your text!" Abigail shouted again. "Read it out."

I turned to look at Susannah, and she looked at me—both of us with wide eyes. I almost giggled, but I turned then and looked at Mama. Her face was white. "Mama?" I whispered.

Mama just shook her head. She took my hand and held it tight.

The meetinghouse remained silent. Reverend Lawson seemed unable to speak. I did not know about anyone else, but I was waiting for someone to tell her to sit down and be still. But Abigail simply stood there, waiting for the reverend to obey her command.

Slowly, then, Reverend Lawson began reading. His voice trembled slightly, though he seemed to get more courage as he went. By the end of the text, he was reading loudly, with courage and conviction.

When he had finished, again Abigail spoke. "That," she said loudly, "is a long text!"

This time, I really had to try hard not to laugh. It *was* a long text! I sneaked a look at Susannah and saw her bite her lip, holding back a laugh.

Abigail turned then, away from the reverend to face the congregation. She looked directly at me. At least, I thought it was me. But when she spoke, it was not to me or about me.

"Look!" she cried out, pointing. "Look at Goody Corey!"

People around us turned, straining their necks to see what there was to see. Since Goody Corey was directly in front of me, I did not have to strain and could see her clearly. She was sitting still, her hands clenched together tightly.

"See her spirit leaving her body?" Abigail cried out. "See? It is above, on the rafters!"

Every eye, I am sure, looked up. Even I could not help looking up at the rafters.

"Sly, is she not?" Abigail said, her own voice sounding sly and bitter. "See? She is on the rafters. And see her yellow bird? It clings to the rafters also."

Goody Corey turned around in her seat. She looked at Mama. Her expression was one of utter dismay and fear. She raised both hands to her chest.

Mama let go of my hand and reached over the pew. She took Goody Corey's hands and held them tightly in her own. "Never mind her," Mama whispered, leaning forward. "Never mind her."

"Oh, oh!" Abigail cried out. "Look, the bird is suckling on her fingers. Now it is on the reverend's hat there on the peg!"

At that, folk leaped onto their feet, and some even ran out of the room. Abigail bent and swayed, and several men stood up and helped lead her away.

Of course, by then the service was over, and we all stood up to leave. Mama linked her arm through Goody Corey's. They spoke together quietly for a moment. I heard Goody Corey whisper something about the judges and heard Mama agree. And then, arm in arm, Mama accompanied Goody Corey out of the meetinghouse. Not another person, except for Susannah and her mama, spoke to Goody Corey—nor to Mama and me. I also noted that no one so much as looked at Goody Corey on the way out. It was as though everyone in the meetinghouse had decided that Abigail had really seen what she had claimed to have seen.

For a few days afterward, the village was quiet, but it was a strange kind of quiet. We were all waiting to see what would result from that strange and terrible time in the meetinghouse. It was even rumored that my very own aunt had begun accusing Goody Corey of tormenting her.

Mama tried to ignore the rumors and continued her work, delivering food to the sick, shopping for goods and foods, and then hurrying home. She reminded me that my aunt and her husband had had quarrels with the Coreys for years and years. My aunt had lost an infant child a while ago, and even for that, she had blamed others—especially Goody Nurse. If godly women were being accused, Mama said, who knew who else could be accused. Therefore, she spoke little to the village folk and made me promise to keep my silence too.

I was terribly distressed. It was so wrong. And there seemed to be no reason! Just because you did not like someone, you could accuse them of witchcraft? There were only two people to whom I could talk—Susannah Bishop, whose parents thought like mine did, and, of course, my friend George. George, however, worried me. Surely he would think like his papa the judge, would he not?

And then, just a few days later, as we expected, another hearing was called. Goody Corey had indeed been accused and summoned to a hearing.

Once again, Papa allowed me to come with him, and once more, Mama refused to come. She said that she would be of no use to her friend there, since the accused were allowed no one to speak for them. Besides, Mama said, she was about to burst with anger and could not trust herself in that place. Papa agreed that if she could not stop herself from speaking out, then she should stay home. As we walked to the hearings, I asked him about it.

"Papa?" I said. "It is very dangerous now, is it not?"

"It is very dangerous. This afternoon, I want you to keep your face as still as your mouth. Can you do that?"

"Yes, Papa."

"Show nothing," Papa said. "No judgment. Nothing. There is so much evil here that even a facial expression can bring trouble to anyone. Speak to no one."

"Susannah?" I asked.

"Yes, you may speak to your friend Susannah, if she

is there."

"George?" I asked. "Can I speak to George?"

Papa took his time in answering. Finally, he said, "I think not. You can speak to him. But you must not speak about this."

I felt a great sadness when Papa said that. George has been my friend forever. Could I really not tell him my thoughts any longer? He would never tell his papa what I had said, would he? But it did not matter, because even though I looked all around the meetinghouse, I did not see George anywhere. I thought that perhaps he had gone back home to help his mama with the spring planting season.

At the meetinghouse, hundreds of people were crammed in. They came, not only from our village, but from neighboring towns. I even saw some of Papa's friends who had come all the way from Beverly, and I wondered how the news had spread so fast.

The session was opened with a prayer by a Salem minister, Mr. Noyes, and when that was concluded, Judge Hathorne turned to Goody Corey. Before a word could even come out of his mouth, however, Ann and Abigail and the other girls began crying out, shouting, and shaking with fits and tremors.

"Look, look!" cried Ann, pointing to Goody Corey. "The devil is whispering in her ear!"

"The man in black takes her aside and whispers.

And she listens!" cried Elizabeth Hubbard.

Goody Corey stared at the girls for a moment, her forehead furrowed. She shook her head, then turned back to the judges. She bowed her head respectfully. "May I have a moment to pray before you question me?" she asked.

"We did not come here to hear you pray," Judge Hathorne answered. "Lift your arms."

Two officers of the court came forward and stood beside her. They lifted her arms, holding them out on each side, then left her to stand there, with her arms outstretched like a cross.

"Keep them that way," Judge Hathorne ordered.

Goody Corey bent her head. She stood there, mute, her arms outstretched.

"What say you to these accusations of evil actions?" Judge Hathorne asked.

"I say I have nothing to do with such actions," she said softly.

"You did not speak with the devil?"

"I have never spoken with the devil."

"It is wrong to lie!" said Judge Hathorne.

"So it is," answered Goody Corey. "But I lie not. We must not believe distracted persons!"

Clearly, she meant the girls. And just as clearly, the girls knew it too. Abigail shouted, "I've been bitten! She bit me."

"She pinched me!" cried Elizabeth.

Goody Corey let her arms drop and put both hands to her head.

At that, Ann put her hands to her head. "Oh, she burns! Oh, the blows to the head."

Goody Corey looked around, with anguish on her face. She twisted her hands together.

Immediately, all four girls twisted and shook their hands, crying out in pain.

"Lift your arms!" Judge Hathorne scolded Goody Corey.

"But I am an old woman!" she cried. "I have no strength."

"You have strength enough to torture these girls!" said Judge Hathorne. "Why did you say the judges' eyes were blinded and you would open their eyes?"

"I said that?" she answered. "I did not say that."

"You said that after service on Sunday," he answered.

At that, I felt my heart thud heavily in my chest. She had said that as she and Mama spoke in the meetinghouse. And Mama had agreed with her. Had others overheard? Had they heard what Mama had said in reply?

"Now will you tell me the truth?" said Judge Hathorne.

Goody Corey nodded. "Yes," she said slowly. "Yes, I remember that now. I did say that. I had forgotten."

"And what else did you forget? The pact with the devil? Do you see how these children are tormented?"

"I see it. But I do not do it."

"Who does it, then?"

"I do not know."

"Do you not believe that there are witches in the country?"

"I do not know that there are any," she replied.

"Did you not know that Tituba has confessed?"

Goody Corey breathed in deeply. She leaned forward against the seat in front of her. Immediately, not just the girls, but Mrs. Pope, who also claimed to be tormented by witches, began crying out in pain. They held their hands to their bosoms, gasping as though they were being pressed hard, their breath sucked out of them.

"Why do you torment these girls?" boomed Judge Hathorne. "Lift those arms!"

"I do nothing!" Goody Corey cried, her voice breaking in despair. "I am a gospel woman."

"A gospel witch!" cried my aunt, Ann Putnam.

And then, Mrs. Pope did something I never thought that I would see a grown person do. She took her muff and threw it at Goody Corey.

It missed and landed on the communion table in front of the judges. For a moment, everyone was still.

And then Mrs. Pope took off a shoe. She lifted it.

And flung it.

It went straight to its target and hit Goody Corey on the head.

Goody Corey cried out and put a hand to her head, where a circle of blood had bloomed on her forehead. She looked down at her hand in disbelief, then looked up at the crowd, fear and terror in her eyes.

The stillness was broken with laughter and shouts. And, though Papa had warned me about keeping my face still and hard, I could not help it. Tears began streaming down my face. How could one of us treat another so poorly—and how could others cheer them on!

My eyes became blinded with tears. Yet when I blinked them away and looked around me, I saw only cold faces, hardened against what they were seeing. I could not flee. I dared not make a scene. But my heart wanted nothing more than to turn and run out of that unholy place.

Chapter Seven

It was two days later that I flung myself into the house, banging the kitchen door behind me, not even stopping to wipe the mud off my feet. I had been out delivering food to Rebecca Nurse again, when I went by the jail and came across something terrible.

"Mama! Papa!" I cried. "Where are you?"

"Elizabeth!" Mama said, hurrying into the kitchen from the hallway. "Your papa has gone into Salem Town for the day. What has happened? Tell me. Quick!"

"Dorcas!" I cried. "Dorcas Good."

Mama sank down into a chair by the fire. She put a hand to her chest. "It is not you!" she said. "Thank the Lord. Sit. Remove your cloak. Wait!"

She got up then and went into the hall where I heard her speaking to Mary Warren. In a moment, they were both back in the kitchen, and Mary bent in close to stoke the fire. Mary has a squint and does not see clearly, though she hears well enough. Mama put a finger to her mouth, shushing me, while Mary went about her work.

I knew why Mama did that. Mary had been seen with Ann and Abigail and the others, and we no longer trusted her. Mama wanted to send her to live elsewhere. It was hard for a young woman to find a place to live if she had no family, and Mary's family had been killed in an Indian raid in Maine. Still, John Proctor was in need of household help, and Papa had already spoken to him about Mary.

When Mary had the fire going again, she nodded to Mama and left the room. Mama motioned me to be still, and she cocked her head, listening. It made a pain grow inside my heart that we did not even feel safe in our own home!

"Mama!" I whispered.

"Wait!" Mama whispered back.

Still tipping her head, she stood and went to the door to the hall. "Mary?" she said. "Did I not ask you to lay the fire in the bedrooms?"

There was no answer, but I heard Mary scurrying up the stairs, and in a moment, Mama returned to the kitchen. She settled in her chair by the fire across from me.

"I feel spied upon by that girl," Mama said. "Now tell me, what of Dorcas?"

"Dorcas is in jail—in jail—and she is only four years old! They accused her of witchcraft, and she admitted it. They took her mama away to that other jail—the one in Salem Town where Sarah Osborne and Martha Corey are, so she is in the village jail all alone. Mama, she is no more a witch than I am."

"Of course not," Mama said. She looked at me. "Move back from the fire," she said. "You are getting overheated."

63

My face was hot, but it was not from the fire. I had been feeling sick for a few days, my throat was on fire, but I dared not tell Mama, or she would keep me indoors. I simply had to be out to do what I could.

"Mama!" I said. "What shall we do?"

"You will do nothing," Mama said. "You will stay right here. I shall go talk to the judges. Judge Corwin has been a friend of your papa's for a very long time."

"No, Mama!" I said. "He will not listen. Please. Let me help. I can talk to George. Do you know what they have done? They have chained Dorcas to a wall."

"Chained her?" Mama said.

"They have, Mama! They say that it is the only way to keep her specter from escaping. It is what they are doing with all of the accused now, chaining them."

For a moment, Mama sat there, staring down at the floor. After a while, she said, "Who be the jail keepers? Do you know?"

"I know one—Papa's friend John Salton. He is kind, I think. I saw his eyes tear when they handed over Dorcas to be chained."

Mama stood and took her cloak from the peg by the door. Mine was still on the chair, spread out by the fire. I could not disobey. But I could change Mama's mind. And I tried.

"Mama," I said. "It will be dark soon. I can handle Papa's saw. The small one. 'Tis no more than a knife."

Mama stood silently a moment. "But where would we keep the child?" she asked, and I almost smiled. Mama is not hard to persuade when she thinks that something needs to be done.

"Why, right here," I said.

Mama tipped her head and looked toward the ceiling, and I knew what she meant: Mary. We could not send her away so swiftly.

"In the barn?" I asked. Though I knew no barn would hold this wild child.

"Perhaps she must stay chained for just a day or two," Mama said slowly. "In that time, we can send Mary away. She knows that arrangements are already being made."

"But Mama! A child in chains? And there are rats in that jail, I have heard it said. And no food."

"We can bring her food."

"No, Mama! Please?"

But just as Mama can be persuaded when she wants to be, she can also be as stubborn as a moose when that pleases her. "No," she said. "You stay here. I will go. I will see what I can do. And I'll bring food too."

"Mama!"

But Mama put up a hand. She came to me. "I promise," she said. "When your papa returns in the morning, if I have not been able to win her release, Dorcas will be freed. Somehow."

I blinked back tears. "Yes, Mama," I said. "But I can hardly bear it."

"I know," she said, and she rested her hand on my cheek. "Why, you are burning up!" she said.

I shook my head. "Just from the fire," I said, and I moved away from her hand.

"I shall be back shortly," Mama said. "Lay the table for supper. Mary will ask a hundred questions. Do what you can to avoid them."

At that, Mama took some cheese and bread from the larder, removed the blanket from the chair by the fire, tucked them all inside her cloak, and was gone into the twilight.

No sooner was she out the door, than the door between the kitchen and the hallway opened, and Mary came in. She carried an armful of bedding, as though she was taking it out of doors to air. But it was already becoming dark, and an icy mist was falling.

"I think I shan't do this now," Mary said, in response to my look. "I will bring these back upstairs."

"Why don't I help you?" I said sweetly. "I know how many times you have been up and down those stairs today." I hoped that she would get the idea that I knew perfectly well that she had been eavesdropping in the hall.

"If you wish," she said.

I took half of the bedding and followed her up

the stairs.

"Where be your mother, so late in the day?" Mary asked as we reached the top of the steps.

"A neighbor needed help," I said.

"What neighbor is that?"

"You probably already know that, do you not?" I said.

"How could I?" she answered.

A small, mischievous part of me wanted to say, "Because you were eavesdropping, and you know it," but of course, I did not.

We lay the bedding back on the beds, then started back to the kitchen. Mary was walking down the steps before me, and halfway down, she turned and looked up at me, her eyes squinting up in that way she has. It is simply poor eyesight, I know, but the squint makes her look mean.

"What think you of the hearings and what they did?" she asked.

I was not sure who she meant—the girls or the accused. But either way, I was not about to answer that question. "I do not know," I replied. "I do not know what to think."

Mary turned back and continued down the stairs. "I know what I think," she said. "This town is afflicted. The devil has made his way in." She opened the door to the kitchen, and I followed her in. "Once we banish the witches, we can find our God again. God has allowed much evil to be set loose in this town. We must purge ourselves and repent."

She went to the fire and added on some wood. Then, without another word, she sat in the chair where Mama had just been sitting. She nodded at me, as though she was expecting me to join her in my place across from her. It seemed, for a moment, that she was assuming the place of my mama, and she had an arrogant look on her face.

I frowned at her. She is only a few years older than I am—seventeen, perhaps. Her face is round and full, but her eyes are narrow, and her hands are dry and cracked. I knew that she had seen her parents killed in an Indian raid right before her eyes. Perhaps that is why her face is mean and hard. I could not imagine seeing such a thing.

"He came to me, too," Mary said now, and for a moment, I thought that she meant the Indians.

"Came to you?" I asked.

"The devil," she answered, her mouth turned up in a smile.

"The devil came to you?"

She nodded. "Right here in this house!"

I simply stared at her.

"He wanted me to sign his book. I refused. But he will be back. He will do anything to attain his goals.

He will use anyone." She smiled at me, her eyes glittering in the firelight. She leaned forward. "He may even be using you!"

This was clearly a threat. And if I had a drop of sense in my head, I would have ignored her, not answered, just as Mama had warned me. But, of course, I have no sense, and so I replied.

"If there be a devil," I spit out, "it is you that he is using! You and Ann and Betty and your silly magic tricks with the dog and the witch cake."

"Who told you about that?" she said, and her hands flew up to her face. She had instantly dropped that superior tone of malice and threat, and for a moment, she looked like the scared girl that she probably was.

"Many speak of it," I answered.

"Who?" she said, still sounding frightened.

"Many," I replied. "And if I were you, I would be careful. You, too, could be accused."

"I?" she said. She laughed. "I shall not be accused."

She said it with such arrogance that I knew—she, too, was part of the plot. She was doing the accusing. And to me, that was one more fact that made me know: this was a dangerous, evil game that had gotten all out of control. But I had seen the fear in her eyes. She knew that I knew about the witch cake and how she and the others had been playing at magic. That gave me some power. I would do all that I could to stop the evil and help the accused.

And right now, Mama was carrying out the first part of that plan.

Chapter Eight

On that terrible night, Mama was able to bring food and a blanket to Dorcas, but she was unable to see Judge Corwin, as he had journeyed to the farm of a friend for the night. I could barely sleep, thinking about Dorcas in jail. Warm in my bed heaped with quilts, and with the fire in the hearth still smoldering, I shivered, thinking of what it might be like to lie chained to a wall in jail. I pictured Dorcas lying on the stone floor, perhaps with rats gnawing at the edge of the blanket that Mama had brought to her.

When Papa returned home the next day, I truly thought that he would have a fit of apoplexy when he heard what the judges had done. And when I told them both what Mary had said to me in their absence, Mama immediately sent her to John Proctor's home to stay. She said there was no sense in letting her spy on our business any longer. And if it meant a bit more work for her and for me without a maid, then we would manage just fine.

It was not until late that day that Judge Corwin returned to town and Papa was able to get a meeting with him. I accompanied him in the cart to the village, bringing food and firewood for Dorcas. Prisoners were given nothing in jail. Food and even firewood had to come from their families, and if they had no families, many starved. Even so, before being released, they had to pay lodging costs for their time in jail, almost as though they had been paying customers at an inn.

Judge Corwin was staying once again at Ingersoll's Tavern, and while Papa went there, I was to go alone to the jail. The jail keeper, John Salton, was a friend of Papa's, and Papa had arranged for me to be allowed in. I was supposed to wait for darkness, however, so that I would avoid being seen by too many village folk. It would not be wise to let others know that I was caring for a "witch." And so, I sat in the cart by the inn, waiting until darkness fell, when I saw a familiar figure approaching slowly.

George! George Corwin. He was coming toward me from out of the dusk, but because of his limp, I recognized him clearly.

"George!" I cried out, so happy to see him. "Here, George!" I called. "I am here."

I clicked the reins of my horse, and we trotted down the street to meet him. "Where go you?" I called. "Will you rest a while?"

George looked up and smiled. "I shall!" he said. "'Tis a cold evening."

He climbed awkwardly into the carriage, a book—perhaps his sketchbook—tucked under his arm. I handed him a heavy blanket to throw over his legs.

72

"George!" I said, when he was seated. "I am so pleased to see you. My papa is visiting with your papa."

"I know," George said. "That is why I am out. They sent me away."

"Why?"

"To talk alone, without me to overhear. Private talk." It was a serious matter, I knew, but still he grinned at me, I think because he was as happy to see me as I was to see him.

"Could you not find a warmer place to get away from them?" I asked. "If I was you, I would have found a place by the fire."

"There is far too much noise," George said. "No place to even sit alone and read in that tavern. And, of course, I cannot sketch in public."

"Your papa still thinks that it is a waste of time?"

George nodded. "I do not even tell him any longer. I do it secretly."

"When will you go back home? I thought that you might have left already?" I asked. "Surely planting time has come?" Of course, I was not so interested in his papa's planting time as I was to find out what else his papa had planned. I desperately hoped that the trials were all behind us.

"We leave in a day or two, at most," George replied.

"Oh, George, I am so happy! Then the trials are over now?"

George shook his head. "I am afraid not. I believe that they are just beginning."

"But you just said you are returning to town!"

"Only because a new court is coming," George said. "There will be a whole new court, arranged by our governor, Sir William Phips. They will hold more formal hearings for the witches."

"You mean those accused of being witches, George."

George twisted the edges of the blanket between his fingers, and I noted that his fingernails were bitten to the quick, the edges bloody and torn. I looked more closely at his face, then. He looked different, his eyes were sunken, and he seemed weary, as though he had not slept for days and days.

"George, what is it?" I asked. "What is happening?"

Before he could answer, a carriage rattled slowly past us, and I kept my head bent until it was past, then I felt angry at myself. Why did I feel like a criminal when I was doing good?

"George?" I said, when the carriage was gone. "What will happen here?"

"More trials, more formal trials. It is called a court of Oyer and Terminer—the highest court in the colony. They are coming with five new judges. You know that your own aunt, Ann's mother, is afflicted by the specters. She has named Rebecca Nurse."

"George!" I cried out. "You cannot believe that! Why, my aunt lost an infant some years ago, and for years, she has blamed Rebecca Nurse for it! She is a disturbed woman, my aunt. Ask my mama. Ask my papa!"

"Elizabeth, how can you be sure that you are right, when so many others see it differently?"

"Because there is no proof, George!" I answered. "How can you and your papa believe that people's spirits leave their bodies and attack others? Where is the proof? The only proof is the word of those disturbed girls!"

"And those women," George added. "They are godly women. They are not simply silly girls. Your aunt is a godly woman."

"And those that they accuse are godly," I answered hotly. "You were with me at Goody Nurse's home. You saw the kind of woman she is."

"Why did she not come to visit the afflicted girls? That is the custom, you know that."

"And you know that she was unwell!" I retorted.

"I know that she said that she was unwell," George answered.

"George!" I said. "George, you know, do you not, that Dorcas Good is imprisoned in there?" I lifted my hand toward the jail.

"I know," George answered. He looked down and

fiddled with the edges of the blanket again. "She admitted to being a witch."

"George! She is four years old!"

George still did not look up. "She showed my father and me the mark on her finger where her familiar sucked. A snake, she said. A little red spot. I saw it myself."

"She sucks her finger, George," I said. "She is a baby. Babies suck their fingers."

George did not answer.

I was so frustrated that I wanted to reach out and shake him. I restrained myself by clenching my fists and taking a deep breath. "George," I said. "Does it not trouble you to keep a child in chains?"

George nodded. "It does trouble me," he said quietly. He sighed and looked up at me. "But, Elizabeth, the devil has powers that we do not understand. He can even take over a little child. I hate it too, don't think I do not. But he has great powers."

"And maybe it is the devil who is making the accusations," I replied, and truly, that is the first time that thought had crossed my mind. But why not? If there was a devil who could do such terrible things, could he not be stirring up all this trouble? Surely good powers were not making such horrible things happen.

George sighed and began awkwardly clambering

down from the wagon. Once on the ground, he looked up at me. "Please, Elizabeth," he said softly. "Please be careful. Do not speak to others as you have spoken to me tonight. You speak too freely."

"What do you mean?" I asked, though I was quite sure that I knew.

"Just be cautious," he said softly. "Please be cautious in what you say." And with that, he turned and went off into the night.

It would be untrue to say that I was not afraid of being accused, but I did know that I had one advantage—I knew about the magic games. I went on to the jail where the jail keeper merely pointed and moved aside so that I could walk down the tiny hallway to where Dorcas was.

Inside that tiny, cold, dark room, Dorcas sat on a cot, her foot chained to the wall, her knees pulled up. Her arms were folded around her, trying to ward off the cold. She was not crying. She simply sat.

I bent down to her. "Dorcas," I said, trying to sound cheerful. "I brought you some food."

She nodded.

"Are you hungry?"

She nodded again. "I am thirsty."

"Good," I said. "I brought you tea and broth and all kinds of good things."

I uncovered the basket that Mama had prepared

and poured some broth into a mug. I held it out to her, and she drank it down without a word. Then she held out the mug for more.

I poured her more, then tore off a hunk of bread and gave that to her along with some deer jerky. She chewed slowly, not ravenously as she had that night in our kitchen. She just seemed tired.

I smoothed her dirty hair as she chewed, trying to untangle the knots with my fingers. "Dorcas," I whispered to her. "Oh, Dorcas."

"Mama is gone," she said.

"I know," I said. "She is in Salem Town. But it is not too far away. They will bring her back."

"My baby is gone."

"I know," I said. "But they will bring her back, too, with your mama."

"No," Dorcas said, shaking her head. "She died."

"Dead? The baby is dead?"

"Yes. She is dead. She died."

"Are you sure? I mean . . ."

I had to look away from her. Tears choked my eyes, my throat. And then, like the big, strong—and foolish—girl that I am, I took Dorcas in my arms, and I cried.

Chapter Nine

They hung Dorcas' mother from a tree in a pasture outside of town. They brought her back from Salem Town jail. They led her along Prison Lane and out to the main street. The cart rattled and shook, and the clippety-clop of the horses' hooves in the quiet day made heads pop out of windows. Soon there was a festive feel as folk began emerging from their houses, crowding and pushing against the cart, jostling each other for the best place to stand and watch. There must have been 100, maybe more.

The guards did little to stop the thrusting and pushing, simply ordering people back, but not doing anything to actually make it happen. Finally, they reached the place where the hanging was to occur. The tree had already been selected. The ladder was in place. They lifted Sarah Good from the cart and stood her on the ground.

It was only then that the crowd became subdued as the minister called on Sarah Good to confess before going to meet her God. She confessed one thing only—her innocence. They put a hood over her head. They tied her arms tight behind her and tied her legs and skirts tightly around her ankles. They lifted her halfway up the ladder and dropped the noose around her neck. She shouted out her innocence. Then the ladder was pulled out from beneath her.

In the days that followed, they hung Susannah Martin, Elizabeth Howe, Sarah Wildes—and Rebecca Nurse.

Papa recounted all of this to Mama and me as we sat close to the kitchen hearth on that summer night, warming ourselves, not only against the chill of the evening, but against the chill inside of our souls. Dorcas remained in jail. She had been imprisoned, in chains, for over one month now. I had been allowed to bring her food daily, but so far, Papa had been unable to win her freedom. George's papa insisted that he could not allow a witch to go free, and my heart was so heavy—so angry at both George and his papa—that I could hardly think straight.

As the weeks had progressed, and more hearings were held, Papa had fretted loudly—to Mama and me—about his inability to put a stop to the proceedings. Many times, he had told us that he planned to take us away from this unholy place, only to change his mind, hoping to be able to effect some changes.

Late one evening, shortly after the hangings, I went with Papa to walk around our grounds. Papa seemed as restless and angry as I was, perhaps even more so. I had never seen him so wild in his emotions. As we walked down the lane to the barns, I was surprised to see the barn door slightly ajar, and inside, several horses were saddled.

"Papa!" I said. "Someone has forgotten to unsaddle the horses!"

"No," Papa said. "Not forgotten."

I looked up at him.

"We will flee to Boston. I have friends there, and from there, if necessary, we can go on to New York."

I just stared at him.

"There are no witch trials in New York," he said.

"Papa!" I cried. I clutched his arm. "Oh, Papa, are you about to be accused?"

"No!" Papa said. "No, I am not. But I truly believe that Jonathan Corwin has gone crazy—he and all the others. A new court is arriving, and who knows what will happen. If a tiny child like Dorcas is in chains, well, who can feel safe?"

"But Papa, why the horses?"

Papa put a hand under my chin and turned me to him. He was smiling, and it made my heart a little easier. "One must be prepared," he said.

I nodded.

"It is simply a wise precaution," he added.

"But you have heard a rumor, Papa?" I asked. "Haven't you?"

Papa shook his head, no.

"But if we flee," I said, "we lose everything! I have

heard they take your house, your possessions, everything. Is it not better to fight back?"

Papa took my arm again, and we resumed our walk. "No, Elizabeth," he said. "You have seen what happens when one fights back. If you admit to being a witch, then you are forgiven. Tituba, you notice, has not been put to death. But if you refuse to admit, they take your life. And remember, I still own my ships. Now, come. Let us go inside with your mama, and no more talk of witches."

"Wait, Papa," I said, tugging back on his arm. "How will we know if we are accused?"

"They do not come with warrants for arrest. They first come to talk. No one has done that yet."

"One more thing, Papa," I said. "What about Dorcas? If we flee, we cannot leave her behind."

Papa sighed and looked away. "I have worried about that, Elizabeth. We will decide that if we need to. Now, come. Let us forget rumors and witches and try to enjoy our supper."

We had come to the kitchen door and met Mama setting the table for supper. We sat and prayed, then ate our meal, each one of us silent, each in our own heads, thinking our own thoughts. And my thoughts were—if we should flee, I must find a way to take Dorcas with us.

I did not sleep much that night, and early the next

morning, before the sun was up, I made my way to the jail, carrying Dorcas' food for the day. The jail keeper, now accustomed to my daily visits, did not bother to keep watch. He was asleep, snoring, his mouth wide-open. I tiptoed past him and down to Dorcas' cell. She lay on her side on the hard ledge, the chain attached to her foot, her finger thrust into her mouth.

I studied the chain and the lock: sturdy and heavy. Though the whole thing hung loosely around her thin, little ankle, I could see that it would not slide over her foot. What then? I could bring a saw, a small one—Papa had plenty of the kind that he used for butchering. But, no, that would take too long and make too much noise.

Dorcas groaned and shifted in her sleep. She could not turn easily, and as she struggled against the chain, I saw the plank give a little where the chain was attached to the wall. Carefully, quietly, I reached across her and tugged on it. Yes, the wall was only wood, rotted and soft. With a good, strong tug, I could pull the chain out of the wall. Could I not? I tried again. Yes, it bulged out when I tugged. There was nothing to do but wait—and hope. If the time came, I could do that. For now, I did all that I could: I took the blanket that Mama had brought to her all those weeks ago and covered her with it. Though it was warm outside, the cell was raw and damp. Beside her, I left the food that I had brought and hoped that the rats would not devour it first.

The jail keeper was still sleeping when I tiptoed past him, and within minutes, I was across the fields and home again. I was just stepping up on the side porch, when a movement caught my eye. I turned. A figure moved away from the shadows by the barn. Who would be out at this hour?

And then I remembered—the horses. Someone was spying on us. Someone saw that the horses were saddled up! My heart thundered in my throat, and I backed up against the porch to avoid being seen. The figure moved away from the barn then and slipped away into the mist.

Before he did, though, I noticed that he moved slowly, awkwardly. Limping.

George. George Corwin. My best friend, George Corwin, was spying on us.

Chapter Ten

There was no need to alert Papa. He was already up, pacing by the front windows. When I told him what I had seen, he seemed angry but unsurprised.

"I was afraid that it would come to this," he said. "Jonathan Corwin has gone crazy, and perhaps his son along with him. Now go, get your mama, and pack up your things. We must be ready to ride and ride hard. Take a warm cloak."

While Mama and I put some things together, Papa paced and muttered under his breath. The sparks of anger that flew from his eyes would have frightened me, had I not known at whom it was directed. We all felt certain then that evil news was on its way that day.

The entire day went by, and no one came. That in itself was strange, because folk in this village often visited each other. It was not until long after dusk had fallen, when it was almost completely dark, that two men came riding into our yard.

"Papa?" I said, when I heard the hooves. "Someone is here."

"Go upstairs now," Papa said. "Have everything ready. We shall flee as soon as possible once they are gone. Should they ask for you or ask you questions, you will say nothing, except what you must. Keep to one word answers if at all possible. Remember, everything that is said can be twisted around. Go to your room now, quickly."

"Yes, Papa," I said. And I fled up the stairs. I did not go to my room, though, but instead crouched at the top, listening, while Mama took her place by Papa's side.

I recognized the men's voices when they came in—two deacons from Reverend Parris' church, Ezekiel Cheever and Edward Corwin.

"What is it that you wish?" Papa asked.

"We come not for you," said Ezekiel Cheever. "We come to speak with your daughter. One of the afflicted has named her. This very day, your daughter's specter attacked her."

I sucked in my breath. *Me? Me?* I was being accused? Of witchcraft? They had come for *me*?

"And who might that 'afflicted' one be?" said Papa.

There was silence then. Silence but for my heart thudding so hard that I knew it could be heard downstairs.

"Mary Warren," Ezekiel Cheever answered.

Mary! Our maid, our former maid?

It seemed then that a part of me broke off and stood apart, laughing. It was so absurd. But then all of me flowed back together again, and I almost cried out. They hanged witches! I was not a witch! I am not a witch!

I could not believe how frightened I felt, the blood

rushing from my head until I felt dizzy and weak. Flee! Flee! But could we?

And then Mama was coming heavily up the stairs, summoning me. "Say nothing," she whispered to me. "Say as close to nothing as you can. Do not get angry, do you hear me? No matter what they say. Simply say yes or no."

"I am not a witch, Mama," I whispered.

Mama rested her hand on my shoulder. "No, you are not a witch," she whispered. "Now, come. I am right by your side. God will be with us. Downstairs we go."

The two men were still standing in the parlor. Papa stood beside them, towering over them, for he is a big man. I could sense Papa's anger in the room, as clearly as if he was shouting and raising his fist. But when he turned to me, his look was calm, and he nodded slightly. I knew what that meant— a reminder of what he had told me earlier. I stopped in the doorway, trembling all over, but I nodded at them politely.

"We have come to speak with you about being a witch," Mr. Cheever said.

I looked up at Mama. She gave me no signal, merely tightened her grip on my hand.

"Have you nothing to say?" Mr. Corwin asked.

"Tell them," Mama said.

"I know not of what you speak. I am no witch," I said.

"Yet Mary Warren claims that it is your specter."

Papa moved then, strode across the room and stood between me and the men. "Elizabeth has answered you," he said, his voice tight with anger. "She has told you that she is no witch. Now, go. And if you have a bit of sense in your heads, you will remember that Mary Warren was a maid in our house. She was so untrustworthy that we sent her away."

"Mary says that Elizabeth's specter wore red," Mr. Cheever replied. "Your daughter wears a red apron this night."

"Mary Warren has weak eyesight. She can barely see, but squints, as you have surely noticed." Papa was moving toward the door as he spoke, ushering the men on their way.

My heart was thundering inside of my chest. I was fearful and angry, and both emotions fought so hard within me that I could barely catch my breath. Mama was holding my hand so tightly that her fingernails dug in, but I did not want her to let go. This was madness. Madness! And now, we must flee our home, our own home! And would we be caught?

When the men were gone, Papa turned to us. "We shall wait an hour or two. They will not be back tonight. But someone may be watching the yard, so it is best to wait." He looked at me. "Elizabeth, you were splendid. Just splendid."

Tears welled up in my eyes. "They say I am a witch! I am not a witch. I am not evil, Papa. I am godly, am I not?"

Papa came to me and wrapped me in his arms. "You are godly," he whispered into my hair. "The only evil in this place comes from them." He held me away from him then. "Now, go, and rest a while. Take a warm cloak, for we shall be riding many hours this night. I will let you know when it is time to leave."

I went up to my room, but I did not settle down to sleep. Even as fearful as I was, there was one thing I could not leave undone. I also knew that I could not ask Papa to do it for me. I waited as long as I could wait, until the house was still and quiet. I knew that Papa would surely not close his eyes and would be watching the yard from a window. But I could go out the side door—the door facing away from the yard, the side closest to the jail. As silently as I could, I ran down the back stairs, out the door, and into the night. I ran across the field, down the narrow lane, praying that the jail keeper would be asleep. If he was not—well, I refused to think about that. And then—glory be—he was asleep in his old chair, his mouth open, his arms dropped down on each side of him, his breath making whistling sounds.

I hurried past him straight to Dorcas' cell. She was awake, sitting up, staring at the wall.

"Dorcas," I whispered. "I am here to take you away."

"I'm thirsty," she said.

I sat down beside her on the cold ledge. "Now, watch this," I said. "And do not make any sound."

I took hold of the chain, pulling hard against the end that was attached to the wall. The wall creaked and gave a little, but the chain did not come loose.

I tried again. It remained attached, but there was a sound—of the bolt coming loose? Or was it rats scurrying in the wall?

I listened, but all was still, and I then tried again. I swivelled around, lifted my skirts, pressed my feet against the wall for leverage, and tugged.

Suddenly, the chain came loose, so quickly that both Dorcas and I fell backward onto the ledge. I grasped her by the wrist before she fell, but not before she cried out.

"Hush!" I said, putting a hand over her mouth. "Hush! I am taking you away, out of here. Not a word."

Her eyes were so wide and her face was so pale that I was afraid she would faint and I would have to carry her.

"Mama?" she whispered. "To see my mama?"

"Yes," I whispered back, because—what else could I say?

I listened some more, my head cocked. All I heard was the light sound of snoring. I peered out into the hall and then, holding Dorcas by the hand, we slipped out of the jail and out into the night.

Chapter Eleven

As we fled through the woods, me holding Dorcas tightly around the waist, I turned and looked behind me. The moon hung low over the horizon, just a sliver in the sky, with a single brilliant star beside it. Dew clung to the grass and the trees and to my skirts as we trotted on. Frogs croaked and a bird called from a treetop and night creatures buzzed all around. But it was only when we came to the outskirts of Boston that my heart lifted.

Salem—beautiful, awful, horrible Salem—was now behind us.

Now flip over and read
George's side of the story!

SALEM WITCH

GEORGE'S STORY

READ ELIZABETH FIRST
THEN READ GEORGE

KINGFISHER
a Houghton Mifflin Company imprint
222 Berkeley Street
Boston, Massachusetts 02116
www.houghtonmifflinbooks.com

First published in 2006
2 4 6 8 10 9 7 5 3 1
1TR/0606/THOM/SGCH/80GSMSTORA/C

LIBRARY OF CONGRESS CATALOGING-IN-PUBLICATION DATA
has been applied for.

ISBN-13: 978-07534-5991-1
ISBN-10: 0-7534-5991-4

Printed in India

MY SIDE OF THE STORY

SALEM WITCH

GEORGE'S STORY

PATRICIA HERMES

KINGFISHER

BOSTON

Have you read Elizabeth's side of the story?
If you haven't, flip back and read it first; if you have,
you can now read George's side of the story!

Author's note:

While this is a work of fiction and the characters of
Elizabeth and George are not based on real people,
much of the dialogue was taken from actual
transcripts of the Salem witchcraft trials, as well
as notes recorded by witnesses at the time.

Chapter One

Darkness had fallen, and the fine mist had turned into ice. I clicked my tongue at Hector, pulling back lightly on the reins, urging him to go slow, knowing how slippery the ground was. Mama would worry if I was out for too long, but there was no sense in hurrying with ice all around. Besides, both Hector and I knew the way and knew how to be careful. Since I do not walk well, Hector has become my feet beneath me.

It was not always so. I could walk as well as anyone until two years ago, when I was kicked by Papa's horse Jeb, and my leg was broken and mangled. I lay in bed for a long time, healing, and when I was finally able to stand, my leg was twisted in a grotesque manner. Since then, I walk slowly with a limp and cannot run around like other boys. But since Papa purchased Hector for me, I can go just about everywhere anyone else can go.

Now, as we made our way carefully home through the icy mist, I looked forward to my time by the fire, talking with Papa and reading. Papa does many things well. He is the owner of many sawmills, but even more important here in Salem Town, he is a judge. Papa hopes that I will become a judge like him when I grow up. He says that if I do well

in school, he may allow my higher education. Though I would like a higher education, I do not wish to study the law. What I would really love to study is art and drawing. Papa, though, has no use for such pursuits. To him, art is just the plaything of the devil. I have a sketchbook, though I pretend to most people that I am taking notes on sermons and such. But when no one is around—when I am alone in the woods—I draw birds and trees and all sorts of wild animals. Mama knows, though she does not tell Papa.

I bent forward against the icy mist, pulling my cloak tighter around me. Hector kept slowing down, looking around, and shying to the side, as though something was frightening him.

"What is it, boy?" I asked, calming him with my voice and my hand on his neck. "Some rabbits? Do you think that spring is coming and there are rabbits for you to chase? Not in this weather, my friend. Now, just over this bridge and over the creek, and we will be home. And I will find a nice treat for you."

He whinnied and began trotting quicker, while I patted him some more. He is truly as good of a companion as any boy or man could want. I sometimes feel that when I speak to him, he knows exactly what I am saying. I told Papa that once, but

6

he scolded me. He said that God put animals in their path and us humans in ours, and we should not stray from such. But I know that he is wrong about that, at least sometimes. When Papa's horse kicked me that day, and Papa took out his pistol and shot Jeb dead, I have never forgotten the look in Jeb's eyes. Surely, at that moment, he knew that he was dying, and yet, he looked up at me, as though saying that he had not meant to hurt me. I had simply been in the wrong place. When you are behind a horse, he does not know what it is you mean to do. It is his own defense.

I shuddered with the memory of that day. And just as I did, Hector reared up, whinnying, his front hooves frantically pawing at the air.

"Whoa! Whoa!" I shouted to him. "What is it? Whoa, boy!"

He settled down on all fours, but kept trotting sideways, shying away from something in the undergrowth. I held on tightly to the reins, holding him back, while I looked around me. Had we come upon a moose, or, worse yet, a bear? Together, we held still, Hector breathing hard, me feeling my heart thudding inside of my chest. I sniffed the air. No bear. Bears have a strong and wild smell, and surely I would have sensed it. What, then?

After a moment, I loosened the reins and clicked

my tongue for Hector to move on ahead. Then, with no warning at all, he reared up high again, his front legs waving in front of him, and he leaped to one side, a little sideways dance. I held on firmly to the reins, but Hector was not able to get his feet under him. He slid sideways and into a hedge, and as he slid, I saw a fox's tail disappear into the undergrowth.

I fell to the ground, sliding backward off his back, over his tail, my foot tangling in the reins. Hector fell too. He slid sideways, then his haunches came down as he slid toward me. I managed to untangle my foot and tried to roll away, but something—a log or a tree root—stopped me. Hector tried to regain his footing, but the ground slid out from under him, the ice crumbling.

And then I was rolling into a ditch and into the creek, and Hector was coming down on top of me. I felt the ice give way beneath me. And that is all I remember for a while.

I do not know how long I lay there. It could not have been long, for if it had been, I would surely have frozen to death. I gradually became aware of where I was—lying in the creek; Hector nearby, munching on some icy grass. I was almost frozen, my cloak and boots soaked through, ice forming on my hair, the fingers of my gloves frozen together.

Slowly, I sat up. "How can you shy away from a

fox?" I muttered to Hector. "Just a fox! You have seen one thousand foxes."

I got my feet under me, then, and pulled myself up. I could tell that I was not hurt too badly, but I was shivering, my teeth chattering wildly. I knew that if I did not get back to the house quickly, I would surely freeze and die out here.

I moved toward Hector, carefully, silently, because sometimes he runs away when he knows that he is not tied or hobbled. I reached for his reins and held on tight, and this time, he did not try to escape from me.

Slowly, painfully, I got my good foot into the stirrups and pulled myself up. He stayed still for me, allowing me to pull my way up to his back, my hands so numb that I could barely clutch the reins. Once up there, my legs were so frozen that I could not hold on tight with my knees, but he let me guide him with the reins. Again, I thought that he was the best horse that God had ever made. Soon, we came around a bend, and never was I so happy to see the candlelight in our front windows.

I stabled Hector and removed his saddle, but I was so cold and frozen that I did not even rub him down. I did give him a handful of oats, though, then made my way to the door and stumbled across the room to the fire.

"George!" Mama cried, turning away from the fire. She hurried over to me. "You are hurt!"

"Not hurt, Mama," I said. "Just almost frozen."

"What happened?" Papa asked.

"Hector stumbled," I said. "He was frightened by something. But it was not his fault!" I added quickly, because I always feared that if Papa got angry at Hector, he might shoot and kill him, just as he had shot Jeb.

"Come," Papa said, "sit." He motioned me to the chair closest to the fire, across from where he sat. "Get those frozen boots off you."

I went and sat, and Papa set aside his book, then bent down and helped me remove my boots. "You are fortunate that you did not freeze to death out there," Papa said, straightening up after a moment.

He handed me a woolen blanket that Mama keeps by the fire, and I wrapped my feet in it. Mama took my soaking cape and spread it out on the hearth, then began preparing some hot broth for me.

"It was a fox!" I said. "I saw its bushy tail disappear into the trees."

Papa frowned at me. "Hector has never been afraid of a fox, has he?"

"No," I said. "He never has. But he was skittish all afternoon. Perhaps from the icy rain."

"Perhaps," Papa said. "Or perhaps something

more evil. I have heard some terrible news. Witches have invaded Salem Village. Even the animals are being affected by the spirits."

"Papa, is it true?" I asked. I have heard similar things in my rides around the village, but I was surprised to hear Papa say so clearly that he believed it.

"Yes," Papa said, nodding at me. "I deeply fear that it is true. I do not know why God has allowed it, but who are we to know the ways of the Almighty? All we know for sure is that the devil has come into Salem Village. Reverend Parris' daughter and niece, Betty and Abigail, have become bewitched. I have been summoned to hear the accusations. Two days hence, we shall go there."

"Who has summoned you? Who are the accused?"

"I would like you to accompany me," Papa added, ignoring my questions. "You will be a judge yourself some day, and you will benefit from being part of this."

"Yes, Papa," I said. "But who makes the accusations? Who are the witches?"

"Names have been mentioned," Papa replied. "When we get there, we will know more. I will not prejudge people."

"But the animals?" I asked.

"Witches have familiars," Papa explained. "They

11

can be animals or birds. The witch takes the form of the animal, just as she takes the form of a human person. Perhaps a witch had taken over the fox, and Hector sensed it. He is a smart animal."

I nodded but said nothing more, I just stared into the fire, thinking hard. I was pleased that Papa said that Hector was intelligent, because I thought so, too. But I did not think much of what he had just said about animals and familiars. I have read the works of Increase Mather, who writes about witchcraft, and I think sometimes, though I would never say it to Papa, that some of it is hard to believe. It is especially hard to believe that witches can take over animals. Yet that is exactly what Papa was suggesting—that the fox I saw was actually a witch. But why would a witch want to harm me? And harm Hector?

Mama handed me some hot broth then, and I took the mug in both hands, feeling the warmth spreading into me. She put a hand on my shoulder. "'Tis a blessing that you were not more hurt," Mama said softly. "A horse should have more sense than to be frightened by a fox."

I smiled up at her, and she returned my smile.

I had a feeling, then, though I could not say for sure, that Mama knew what I was thinking—and that she, too, wondered whether the stories of

witchcraft were truth. But in a day or two, we would all know more. For now, all that mattered was that I was home with my family, warm and safe by the fire, and any evil that there was, at least for now, was outside our home.

Chapter Two

The next morning, Papa had business to attend to in Boston. When he returned home that evening and we were sitting by the hearth, we were startled to hear a horse galloping down the lane. Whoever it was seemed to be in an incredible hurry, and I looked up at Papa.

Papa got to his feet. He motioned to Mama to stay back while he went to the door. When he saw who it was, he opened the door wide. The person who appeared at our door was soaked with rain and ice and breathing hard. It was only when he stepped inside and pulled off his hat that I recognized him—George Burroughs, the Reverend George Burroughs, Papa's friend after whom I had been named.

I rose to my feet, but he motioned for me to sit.

"No, no," he said. "No need." He turned to Mama then, who was holding out her arms for his wet cloak and hat. She took his things and began spreading them out by the fire.

Papa pulled another chair close to the fire, and Reverend Burroughs sat down while Mama hurried to bring him some hot cider.

He thanked Mama, and then he said, "I bring terrible news. Terrible, terrible news."

"We have heard," Papa said. "Witchcraft. And

the devil."

"Witchcraft? No, Indians!" Reverend Burroughs said. "Devils themselves! They have destroyed the entire town."

"Salem?" Mama cried. "Salem Village?"

"No, no," Reverend Burroughs replied. "York. York, Maine. I have just come from there. So many of them killed, hacked to death. Evil men!"

Papa made a motion to Mama then, a small nod of his head. I knew what he meant. It was a motion that I had seen before—for Mama to leave the room. There are many things that are not appropriate for women to be part of, Papa always says. Women's minds are not as strong as the minds of men.

I am not quite so sure of that as Papa is, for I have seen very strong minds in women—or girls, at least—such as my friend Elizabeth Putnam. But of course, I do not speak these thoughts aloud.

Mama nodded, gathered her skirts around her, and picked up her sewing basket. When she had left the room, Reverend Burroughs continued. He described the most horrific scene imaginable—Indians creeping through the snow before daybreak, scaling the walls of the garrisoned town, invading the homes. They burned and slaughtered everyone that they met—children, too. It was snowing heavily, and on and on they came. Those that they did not

15

slaughter, they kidnapped.

In my head, I could see the horror of it—hundreds of Indians, silently creeping through the town, carrying torches, burning the houses, babies crying out for their mothers.

"Some of the children were cut up and slaughtered before the eyes of their parents," Reverend Burroughs went on, and he sat back in his chair, his eyes closed against what he must also have been seeing inside of his head.

"The houses were garrisoned?" Papa asked. "No militia came to help?"

"Yes, they came, and far too late!" Reverend Burroughs answered. "Captain Floyd and his men got there, but the town was already destroyed."

Burned up and gone. Not a soul left.

The three of us sat silently for a while. A part of me wanted to cry. But I am almost a man. Yet how can one hear such news and not want to cry? I looked across the hearth at Papa, and he, too, seemed stunned by the news.

After a moment, Reverend Burroughs spoke again, his voice still trembling with anger. "These fiends do not care at all for life nor for God. They are savages, every one of them."

"Perhaps," Papa said. "Yet we must not abandon them to the devil."

"Abandon them to the devil? They are devils themselves!" Reverend Burroughs exclaimed, and I felt a bit surprised by how distracted and angry he sounded. "What have we done that God is showing His displeasure against this land? He set His hand to help us but now writes bitter things against us."

"Yes," Papa said. "Yes. I fear that you are correct. You know, do you not, about the accusations of witchcraft in the village? It is one more sign of the devil's work."

"I have heard. I have even seen the girls," Reverend Burroughs said. "In the very house where once I lived."

Papa nodded, and I remembered that Reverend Burroughs had been the minister before Reverend Parris came to the village.

We sat quietly. A log shifted in the fire, and red embers flared up. I thought about Papa's words, and the words of Reverend Burroughs. Had God truly turned away from us? Were witches God's way of punishing us for evil things that we had done? But what kinds of evil?

I felt guilty then, my thoughts turning to evil that I had done. I knew that my mind had been idle as I rode Hector through the woods. Should I have been praying, not spending time daydreaming, sketching trees and birds and squirrels and foxes? Is that why God had caused the Indians and witches to attack?

17

I looked at Papa and at Reverend Burroughs.

"Will you stay here tonight?" Papa asked Reverend Burroughs then.

Reverend Burroughs stood up and shook his head no. "I am staying at Ingersoll's Tavern this night," he replied. "But I thank you for your hospitality."

He began to take his leave, then he turned to me. "You are looking well enough," he said.

"Yes, sir," I replied. "I am feeling well."

"You were not grievously hurt?" he asked.

"Hurt? My leg? It sometimes aches, in bad weather." I smiled. "It seems to be bad weather all of the time now."

"But were you not hurt in the woods last evening?"

He could not mean my fall last evening. No one could have heard of it yet. I just looked at him.

"You were thrown by your horse?" Reverend Burroughs persisted. "And fell into the creek?"

"Yes, sir," I replied. "That did occur."

I felt that it would be rude to ask how he knew, so I said nothing, though my heart was hammering wildly.

"I stopped by the Parris' house to give them this news. Abigail spoke of it, so did Betty," he said.

"But who would have told them?" I asked.

"They said it was Tituba. She told them that a fox had run across your path. I am glad that you are not

18

injured. But those girls are grievously tormented."

Papa did not speak, but he looked at me. In his eyes, I saw what he was thinking: it was true. The fox was her familiar. A witch had attacked me.

Later, when Reverend Burroughs had left and we had all retired to our beds, I lay awake a long while, thinking. I thought about witch attacks. I thought about Indian attacks. I thought about my own daydreaming, my sketching, and how I was wasting my time. And where last night I had thought that all the evil was outside our walls, I now feared that God's anger had moved into our home. More than anything, I feared that in some way, I was to blame.

Chapter Three

By the next morning, Papa and I were settled at Ingersoll's Tavern. It was noisy in the extreme, village folk and strangers, too—some from miles away—were all there to attend the witch hearings that were to be held right in the tavern. After my talk with Papa the evening before and the business about the fox, I was seriously afraid. If a witch had truly attacked me, I wanted to learn why I had been singled out and what I had done to make Tituba—and God—angry at me.

Many people in the tavern murmured seriously among themselves about the accusations by the Putnams, clearly convinced that the accusations were true. However, I could tell that some merely thought that it was entertainment. A small part of me—and here, I am ashamed to admit it—was rather thrilled about it too. However, after a time of all the fuss and conversation in the tavern, I was restless and longed for a quiet place to sketch. Papa, perhaps sensing my dismay, though misunderstanding it, sent me out of the tavern to get him some tobacco twists. So, though I would much rather have been given a quiet place to draw and think, I was glad to get away. But thinking about my idleness, and God's anger, I had begun to wonder if I would ever sketch again.

On my way to the shop, I met my friend Elizabeth and accompanied her to the house of Goody Nurse. As we do not see each other often, it was an unexpected delight to see my dear friend. But our conversation, usually easy and full of laughter, left me with a sense of unease. Elizabeth is determined that there are no such things as witches, and she tells everyone that she meets. Although I respect, even enjoy, her independence, often I am angry at her foolishness. Even when I told her that it was her own aunt who was making the accusations, she still laughed. As I walked back to the tavern with Papa's tobacco twists, our conversation echoed in my head.

"How can folk believe in such nonsense?" Elizabeth had said. "Ann and her mama and papa are always accusing neighbors of all sorts of things. Last time they came to court, it was because someone's cattle had broken through their fence and was grazing on their land. All it really was was one silly, little cow munching some silly, little grass."

I had warned her that it was not silly cows but the work of the devil. And then, something mean had come over me. Perhaps I was angry at the scornful way that she spoke, or perhaps I just wanted to impress upon her the seriousness of others people's concerns. Or maybe I was simply showing off. But

when I turned to go, I had said, "Yes, I do think that there are witches. I do believe that the girls are tormented. There were just Indian attacks, and an entire town has been destroyed. I agree with Reverend Burroughs that God has turned against our land. It would be good if you were to listen."

And, as I made my way back through the sleet, I am ashamed to say that I felt a great deal of anger in my soul. It was cold and icy out of doors, the wind howling through the bare branches of the trees. Above me, the ice-coated branches whipped back and forth. Occasionally, I heard a snapping sound as a branch or twig was spun off a tree, sometimes landing in the branches of another tree, sometimes falling sharply to the ground in front of me. It was a fierce and deserted landscape out there, and I could believe that it was the territory of witches. Men back at the tavern were suggesting that the weather itself had been brought on by the witches. And, why not? If a witch was capable of bringing evil, surely she could bring evil weather.

On the following morning, Papa began the proceedings in the main room of the tavern, sitting next to Judge Hathorne. The tavern was even more crowded than it had been on the previous day—men and women and even small children were all crammed in. The noise was so great, and the crowds

were so unmannerly, that it seemed as if nothing could be accomplished. People pushed, shoved, stepped over others in their way, doing whatever they could to get close to the accused. It was then that Papa and Judge Hathorne decided that the meetinghouse would be more suitable. It was much larger, and there would be many more seats. Papa also said that it was more appropriate, since it was a place of God, and so it was more suited to such an important and serious undertaking.

Looking around at the crowds as we made our way down the street, it seemed to me to be not so much a serious mood as it was a jolly mood. In the crowd were the girls who were doing the accusing—Ann Putnam, Betty Parris, Abigail Williams, and a girl whom I had not previously known as an accuser, Elizabeth Hubbard. There were also the accused witches—Sarah Good, Sarah Osborne, and the maid Tituba. But even so, everyone mingled, men talked and laughed among themselves, and though some, especially the women, seemed serious and prayerful, many more seemed to be in the mood of a festivity. I could even hear laughter and joking. Because I walk slowly, I was occasionally jostled, almost overrun, as people thronged around me, pushing their way ahead.

When we finally arrived at the meetinghouse, people fought their way in, stepping over each other to find seats, or even a place to stand, as close to the accused as possible. Papa found a place for me in the front near the communion table that was to be used as a judicial bar, and he gave me a small book in which to write. He wanted a record of the proceedings, and I was honored he thought that I was capable of such an important task.

When all who could fit were finally crammed in and the judges were settled again, Reverend Hale opened up with a prayer. He begged the Lord for enlightenment to help us find and remove those who sided with the devil. It was a serious prayer, and I tried to scribble down the precise words so as to leave nothing out. I also fervently added my own prayers to his.

Papa opened by speaking to Sarah Good first. "Sarah Good!" he boomed out, and my heart swelled to hear how strong and commanding he sounded. "What evil spirit have you familiarity with?"

Sarah Good did not seem at all moved by the seriousness in his voice, nor even by the seriousness of the hearings. "Evil spirit?" she replied, and though she did not laugh outright, there was laughter in her voice. "None!"

"None?" he repeated.

"None!" she replied. She looked directly at him, her eyes defiant.

"Have you made no contract with the devil?" Papa asked.

She smiled outright then. "No," she replied. "No contract with the devil nor anyone else."

"You are aware, are you not," Papa asked, "that you are accused of the most heinous of crimes and sin?"

"I am aware of that. I am not guilty of that."

"Why do you hurt these children?" Papa asked, sweeping his hand toward the girls.

"I do not hurt them!" she replied.

A voice from the meetinghouse floor suddenly shouted out. "Watch her!"

We all turned. There, standing toward the back, was Sarah Good's husband—her very own husband—and he was pointing at her. "Yea," he went on. "She either is a witch, or she shall be soon!"

There was stunned silence, and we all stared at him.

"Tell us what you know," Papa said, addressing William Good. "Come up here. Tell us what signs you have seen."

William Good shuffled his way to the front. He is an unkempt man, and he stood for a while with his shaggy head bent downward. When he spoke, he did not even lift his head to look around him, and he spoke so quietly that I was sure that few

people except the judges and I who were closeby, could hear. "Her bad carriage to me is a sign," he muttered. "Her conduct is evil. She is an enemy to all that is good."

"You know that?" Papa asked.

"I know that," he answered.

Papa and Judge Hathorne bent their heads together to confer. I saw Papa nod.

And then Judge Hathorne turned to the girls. "I desire for all of you," he said quietly, gravely, "to look upon this woman, Sarah Good. And tell us—is it she who torments you?"

The girls turned. They lifted their eyes and looked at Sarah Good.

"It is!" gasped Ann Putnam.

And then, with no warning, and almost simultaneously, all four girls began to dance. At least, that was the first thought that came into my head. They swayed, their feet tapped, their arms flailed. They twisted themselves into the most grotesque contortions that anyone could imagine. Betty Parris' arms were flung above her head and then flung behind her back in such a way that it seemed impossible for her to be human. Her eyes rolled back in her head, and her tongue came out.

Alongside her was Ann Putnam. Fearful sounds came out of her, and her tongue also flew out of her

mouth, in and out, back in and out again. All four girls were contorted and crying out, as the rest of us looked on in awe and desperate fear. I realized then that only an outside force could possibly toss the girls around like that.

I looked back at Sarah Good. A filthy look had crept onto her face. She sneered at the girls and shook her head, smiling widely.

"You do this to them?" Papa shouted over the uproar.

She gave him an amused look. "No," she said. "No, I do not."

"Then how do you explain it?" Judge Hathorne asked.

At that, Sarah Good bent her head, her eyes cast downward. She was silent for a while, a long while, as though she was thinking. I wondered—could it be that she was asking for forgiveness for what she was doing? But when she looked up, it was only to send a withering look at her husband. And then she said, " 'Tis not me. 'Tis Sarah Osborne who is doing it."

I was writing as fast as I could, because Papa had wanted me to record everything—not just the words and actions of the accused and the accusers, but all that was happening in the courtroom—laughter, sounds, shouts, everything. But I could hardly keep up, for the courtroom at that moment turned into

total chaos. Men called out accusations and threats, and in order to bring calm, Papa ordered that Sarah Good be removed from the meetinghouse.

It took quite a while for things to settle down, and those moments gave me an opportunity to catch up with my note taking. Once order was restored, Papa addressed Sarah Osborne, and I was able to listen and follow along again.

"You heard that you have been accused by yet another," Papa said. "What say you to these accusations?"

"She said this morning that she was more likely to be bewitched than that she was to be a witch!" A man's voice called out. "And she said she would not be tied to that lying spirit man anymore."

Again, we all turned to see who was speaking, and again, we viewed something appalling. This, man, too was a husband—the husband of Sarah Osborne.

"You have heard your husband," Papa said, turning back to Sarah Osborne. "Why say you that? Who is this lying spirit man? The devil? Have you been bewitched?"

"It was but a dream," she replied. "I have not been bewitched. I did dream of a man like an Indian. He was all in black when he came to me. He did pinch my neck and pull me to the door of the house as though he would drag my body out of

doors to slay me."

"That was the devil?" asked Judge Hathorne.

"No. No," she answered. "Black, like an Indian."

And I immediately thought of Reverend Burroughs and the Indian attacks in York, Maine. Did the Indians not drag folks from their homes? It seemed almost as though Sarah Osborne had been there, had seen it. Or could it be that the Indians and witches worked together?

"But she has not been to meeting in many months," cried her husband again. "Over a year. Far more than a year."

I stared at Alexander Osborne, then at his wife. Fear and confusion filled my heart. Were both women witches? It could not be possible, could it? Was this simply a way for the men to rid themselves of women that they thought were unworthy wives? I could not even imagine Papa saying such a thing about Mama. Unless . . . no, a witch could not take over our household, my very own mama. Yet a witch had attacked me!

With all these thoughts scrambling around in my head, I again fell behind in my note taking. But I soon had an opportunity to catch up, because Judge Hathorne and Papa bent their heads together to confer once again.

After just a little while, they both nodded, and

Judge Hathorne looked up. He pointed at Sarah Osborne. "Look upon this woman," he ordered the girls. "Raise your eyes and look upon her."

Silence fell on the meetinghouse. Every one of us, I am sure, held our breath. I could barely make myself look, fearful that I would see the same horror and torments that had happened when they looked at Sarah Good.

Slowly, each one of the girls turned. Each one looked at Sarah Osborne. Sarah Osborne did not turn away. She boldly returned their looks.

Ann Putnam began to shudder. Abigail began to sway and moan. All four girls fell into fits again. All four of them fell to the floor, shaking, quivering, calling out, rolling around in agony and torment.

"What say you to this?" shouted my papa over the din and noise of the girls' torments.

"I cannot help it!" Sarah Osborne shouted back. "I cannot help it if the devil takes my form and goes about in my likeness to hurt these girls."

And she turned away from them, shaking her head as though she was disgusted with them and what they were doing.

I, though, was not simply disgusted. I was terrified. For I suddenly had a terrible thought: since a witch had already chosen to attack me, was it not possible that she could also take over my body? Could I, too,

be tormented, tossing and twitching and jerking, just as these girls were being tormented? I prayed not. I fervently prayed that God would protect me from the terrible evil and torments that I was witnessing.

Chapter Four

A few nights later, I went with Papa and Reverend Lawson to the home of Samuel Parris. Reverend Lawson had been the pastor of our village church before leaving for Boston, but he had come back when he heard the dreadful news of what was happening here. After the wild and horrific scenes of possession of the past few days, Papa and Reverend Lawson thought that by praying with Reverend Parris, they could bring some calm and peace to Abigail and Betty.

That is what they told each other. But Papa also had another thought in mind. He told me privately that it was his chance to speak with the girls, Betty and Abigail, and to be sure of the truth of what they claimed. He said that false accusations were as bad as false confessions and he wanted to be absolutely sure that the girls were not lying or pretending, before going on to the ultimate result of these hearings—the death by hanging of the witches.

We were welcomed by Reverend Parris and shown into the parlor. There, sitting in that cold room by the meager burning fire, was Abigail. She seemed solemn and sad, though she smiled and nodded graciously at us. Betty, however, was not there, having gone with her mama to Boston for a rest.

It struck me as strange that Betty would leave just when the trials were beginning, but Reverend Parris said that she was in great need of rest, great need to be removed from this horror. Well, then, I thought, why did they not also send Abigail for a rest? That was clearly none of my business, though one look at Abigail, and one could see that she, too, was exhausted.

When we had been seated, we bent our heads and sat silently for a while.

"God has singled us out," Reverend Lawson said solemnly, "by giving to Satan to range and rage among us, and we must . . ."

Abigail leaped up from her seat.

Startled, we all looked up.

"Whish!" she cried. "Whish!" She threw her arms up above her head. "Whish, whish!"

And then, like a demon possessed, she began virtually flying around the room, around and around in circles, shouting, screaming over and over again, "whish, whish!" Her eyes were closed, and she rammed into walls, bounced off them, raced back in circles again. Back and forth across the room she went. At one point, it seemed as if she would throw herself into the fire, but Papa jumped up and stood in front of the hearth, his entire body blocking her way. He reached for her, threw his arms around

her, but she was stronger than he was, and she tore herself away from his hold. Once again, she began circling the room.

"Whish!" she shouted. "Whish!"

"Abigail!" Reverend Parris cried, leaping onto his feet. "Abigail!"

He ran to her side, but she darted away from him, her feet as quick as a deer. She flung herself against the far wall, waving her arms violently like a trapped bird.

"Whish!" she cried. "Whish!"

At that, Reverend Lawson also leaped onto his feet, and all three men followed her, reaching out for her, but she had the swiftness of a sprite, a devil, and ducked away from their hands.

"Whish, whish!" she yelled. She seemed to me like a bird suddenly finding itself trapped in a house or a barn. Around and around the room she went, all three men reaching for her, each one missing her at the last moment.

Then, just as Papa seemed about to catch her, she threw herself against the fireplace. There was a dreadful noise as her head cracked against the hearth, and I could see that it was only because she was stunned that Papa was able to hold her still.

"Abigail, Abigail!" Papa cried, and he wound his arms tightly around her.

All this time, I was simply sitting still, for I was not only too shocked to move, but I knew that I was far too clumsy to be able to catch her.

Abigail seemed to be subdued and quiet for a moment in Papa's arms. She breathed deeply and looked at me then. And then, suddenly, violently, she twisted away from Papa's grasp and threw herself across the room and straight onto my lap, alighting there like an enormous bird. "Whish!" she cried again.

"Hold her!" Papa shouted. "Hold her!"

I did. I wrapped my arms tightly around her, while she continued to struggle hard against me. I am very strong in my arms, as a result of having to use them more than I use my legs, but even so, it took all of my strength to restrain her. She had enormous power, the force of the devil, perhaps.

"Whish!" she cried again, but her voice became smaller then, pitiful, like a child. "Whish?" She breathed in deeply, and she seemed to relax, sinking back against me.

"Abigail!" Papa said then, bending close, as I loosened my hold on her slightly. "Abigail, can you hear me?"

"I hear her!" Abigail said.

"Yes?" Papa said. "Who?"

Abigail began crying, turning her head this way

and that violently, and again I strengthened my hold on her. "No, I shall not. No, I shall not! I shall not sign the book!"

"What book?" Papa asked.

"The devil's book!" Abigail replied, looking up at Papa, then turning to me, her eyes wide, her teeth bared like an animal at bay. "I will not, I will not!"

Suddenly, she cried out again, "No!" In an instant, she had twisted herself out of my grasp, leaped away from me, and ran toward the fire once again. She bent down. She grabbed a firebrand, two firebrands, with her bare hands and flung them around the room.

One landed in a corner by the window, and the other came perilously close to hitting Papa in the head. At that, all three men, Papa and Reverend Lawson and Reverend Parris, converged at the hearth. Together, they were finally able to catch and hold her. I scurried to the corner and retrieved the firebrand that was smoldering and smoking, tossing it back into the fire before it could set the house ablaze.

My heart was racing violently inside my chest, and my breathing was coming fast. How could God permit this? How could God allow the devil and witches to torment us in this way? For there was no doubt that this was not theater. Abigail was

tormented, grievously.

"Tell us, Abigail," Papa said, when they had her settled down, all three men still holding onto her. "Who is tormenting you in this way? Tell us. We can help you if we know."

"Goody Nurse!" she cried. "Goody Nurse! But I shall not sign the book."

Goody Nurse. I had visited Goody Nurse with Elizabeth. Could a friend of Elizabeth's really be tormenting Abigail in this way? No. She seemed like a godly woman.

"Abigail?" Papa said, as Abigail seemed to relax and breathe more normally. "Abigail, how be you?"

"Tired," Abigail answered, breathing deeply.

"Can you sit now?" Papa asked.

She nodded, and the men released her. I watched her with fear, however, not at all sure that she would not begin to fly around the room again. But it seemed as if she would be still for a while, because she slumped down like someone who was exhausted.

"Who tormented you so?" Papa asked again. "Tell us now."

"Goody Nurse," replied Abigail, looking up at Papa. "She thrust the devil's book at me. She ordered me to sign, but I would not. And so she tormented me. Her sister rode behind her."

"Her sister?" asked Papa.

37

"Goody Cloyse," Abigail answered.

Reverend Lawson looked at Papa. Papa looked back.

"Goody Nurse is a good woman, a godly woman?" Reverend Lawson asked. "And her sister, Goody Cloyse, also?"

"Both churchwomen, yes," Revered Parris responded. "But let none build their hopes of salvation on simply being church members. The devil cares not about that as he roams our village."

After a while, when it was clear that Abigail's fit was over, we took our leave, Papa and me, leaving the preachers to continue to pray with Abigail. On our way back to Ingersoll's Tavern, where we were staying for the duration of the hearings, Papa and I did not speak much. I was so absorbed in my thoughts and the horror that I had seen that I could not think of what to say. Never could I have imagined the evil that could flow from the devil. I do believe that seeing it with my own eyes was necessary. It made me think of the terrible torments that Cotton Mather had written about, of witch attacks on Martha Goodwin. She, like Abigail, had been drawn to the fire to throw herself in. To witness Abigail being tempted again and again to sign the devil's book was something that moved my soul to resolve. I now knew that my task was to help Papa in every way that I could to bring the witches to trial. And to see them hanged if such was God's will.

Chapter Five

The next morning was Sunday, a day for meeting and for prayer. It was also a sacrament Sunday. As Papa and I walked to meeting together, Papa wondered aloud to me who would be taking the sacrament.

"Do you think, Papa," I asked, "that witches will try and partake?"

"I think God would prevent that," Papa said. "But I know not. I have never been in such dire situations before. Let us attend meeting and listen to some holy words. I believe our souls need comfort and strength."

I smiled at Papa. "I know my soul needs it," I said.

Papa put a hand on my shoulder for a moment—a rare gesture—and then we made our way inside.

The meetinghouse was crowded, though not as crowded as it had been for the hearings. I saw Abigail Williams and a few others whom I recognized. Abigail seemed much calmer than she had been the night before, and she even sent a small smile my way when she saw me looking at her. I also saw Sarah Cloyse, the woman that Abigail had mentioned as one of her tormentors. Would Sarah Cloyse dare try and take the sacrament?

Across the aisle, I saw Elizabeth sitting alongside her mama, and my heart leaped with joy. I knew

that Elizabeth still did not believe that there were such things as witches, but I also knew that if she had seen what I had seen last evening, she would be convinced. Still, knowing her and how strong her opinions are, I bent my head in prayer that she would be enlightened.

When the service began, Reverend Parris immediately addressed the concern that was on every single mind, though he did not speak of Abigail's torments directly.

"Occasioned by the dreadful witchcraft broke out here," he said, "with two members vehemently suspected of being she-witches, our discourse today will be on John 6:70."

He paused and looked around the congregation. I slid a look at Papa. I do not know my Bible as well as I should, and I wondered if Papa knew what that reading was. But Papa was not looking back at me.

Reverend Parris continued his silence, contemplating the congregation for what seemed like a long time. There was utter silence in the meetinghouse. Who were the two women to whom he referred? Did he mean Goody Cloyse? Did he mean Goody Nurse? Or did he mean Sarah Good and Sarah Osborne, who had already been accused? I think that every person in the meetinghouse was pondering the same questions, for there was an

awesome silence. I wondered if there were those in the congregation, witches, whose consciences were pricking them, begging them to confess and to be pardoned. If I had not been almost grown, I think I might have reached out for Papa's hand.

"Listen now," Reverend Parris went on finally. "Listen, as he speaks as the Lord our God: 'Have I not chosen you twelve, and one of you is a devil?'"

Suddenly, right in front of me, a woman stood up. She turned away from the front and turned to face the back of the meetinghouse. It was Goody Cloyse. Her mouth was pulled up tight, her cheeks pale. Even from where I sat, I could see that she was trembling. From anger? From fear?

Again, I glanced at Papa, who was staring at Goody Cloyse, along with almost everyone else in the congregation. Even Revered Parris had paused and was watching her.

She made her way past the worshippers alongside her. People moved aside. Once she was in the aisle, she looked neither right nor left. She strode down the aisle to the back of the church. I could not help it. I turned to watch. At the back, she flung open the door. She strode out into the cold. And slammed the door violently behind her.

A witch? I looked at Papa. His mouth was pulled into a tight line. A witch, who was showing her

disdain for all that was holy.

When the service had concluded, I made my way outside with Papa. Many people were gathered in the cold, whispering and murmuring among themselves. Papa went to speak with Reverend Parris, and I looked around for Elizabeth. She was standing alone, waiting while her mama spoke with some other women, and I hurried to her side. "Was that not dreadful, Elizabeth?" I said. "The way she stormed out? Do you . . ."

But Elizabeth did not allow me to finish. "So you are still here, then?" she asked coolly. "I am surprised to see you."

I knew from her tone that she was still upset from our encounter last week—when we had met outside the jail, and I told her that the trials would continue. Elizabeth was hoping that there would be no more hearings, no more trials. But that was not to be.

"We are going back soon," I answered. "But not until five new judges arrive for the high court, the court of Oyer and Terminer, to hear the witch trials."

"Witch trials," Elizabeth murmured, shaking her head.

For a moment, I did not answer. How could I charitably deal with this—knowing what I knew, with my best friend not believing? Yet I knew that

it would be cowardly to avoid answering her, cowardly before my God. If she had only seen what I had witnessed with Abigail this past evening.

"Elizabeth," I said. "Listen to me. The devil is abroad in this town. Reverend Parris sees it. I saw it last night! Why can you not? There are many, many witches doing evil!"

"Accused witches," she answered.

"Accused witches," I replied. "But Elizabeth, these are credible accusations. Really. I saw Abigail being tossed around in the minister's house last night, dreadfully tormented."

"You saw it?" Elizabeth asked.

I nodded.

"And did she not just love the attention that you gave to her?" Elizabeth said.

"Elizabeth!" I said. "Why do you continue to defend Goody Nurse and all the other witches—when they afflict your very own aunt?"

"My aunt by marriage only!" Elizabeth said. "Oh, George, how can you believe this foolishness?"

"How can you not believe?" I retorted. "How can you be so sure when everyone else sees what I see?"

"Not everyone!" Elizabeth answered. "You know that Goody Nurse is a holy, godly woman. You must see that. And George!" At this, she put a hand

gently on my arm. "Why does your papa keep Dorcas Good chained up in the jail still? She is just a baby, George!"

I nodded. It truly was sad. But as Papa has said, the devil can take over anyone's body if that person allows it. "I know, Elizabeth," I answered. "But she has admitted being a witch. She was not simply accused. She admitted it."

Elizabeth looked around for her mama, who was still speaking seriously with some others. She turned back to me. "Dorcas is a child, George," she said.

"Perhaps," I said. "But she is also a witch."

Elizabeth just shook her head and smiled. For some reason, her calm manner and her smile made me more despairing than if we had had an actual argument. It also made me angry. I could not understand how someone I loved could not see what I saw.

"I pray that the devil does not visit you, Elizabeth!" I said, trying not to show my anger.

Elizabeth began moving toward her mama. Before she went, though, she turned back to me. "I am afraid," she said softly, "that he has already visited you!"

Chapter Six

Perhaps it was the warmth of the new spring, of tiny, pale leaves and budding trees that made my heart feel easier for a little while. Certainly, as the spring approached, there were still many accusations and many manifestations of witches. One day, Abigail had even witnessed a witch gathering, where the witches celebrated a sacrament with red bread and red wine and tempted others to partake. It had taken place in a pasture beside her uncle's house, and, according to her, many attended. Mercy Lewis, who had been there, said that she was tempted again and again to partake of this hideous sacrament. She turned her head away and refused.

And yet, in spite of all that had happened and was still happening, my spirits soared on some mornings, as the sun rose earlier and earlier, warming the earth. Papa and I had taken up residence in Salem Town, where the new court would do business, but we returned to our home frequently so that Papa could attend to his own business. It was there at home, with familiar things and Mama's sweet face, that the horror of the witch happenings seemed to recede. It seemed that sometimes, during those early weeks of spring, that those horrid events had never even happened.

On some days, I was able to saddle up Hector and ride in the woods, my sketchbook once again tucked into my saddlebag. Riding in that way gave me time to think. The witch events were so dreadful, and the images of possession so appalling, that in the midst of it, one could lose all sense of what was real and what was not. I thought about all of that during my rides through the woods. And as I rode, there was one part of this business that worried me more than anything else: it was that all of our belief in the witches was only based on the words of the girls. No one else had seen what they claimed to see. Elizabeth had remarked on that again and again. And thinking of Elizabeth suddenly made me want to go and visit with her. I did not want to argue with her. I did not want to try and persuade her to my way of thinking. I just wanted a chance to talk with her, to enjoy her friendship once again.

And so, one warm afternoon when my chores were finished, I saddled up Hector and rode back into Salem Village. I went slowly, enjoying the scent of trees beginning to bloom, enjoying the feel of the saddle beneath me, Hector reacting to the spring as if he was a colt again. He bounced sideways here and there, not spooked as he had been that terrible winter night, but bouncing playfully. We saw rabbits

and foxes and, once, we even sniffed out a bear, that raw, heavy, dusky smell of a bear awakened from its sleepy winter den. It did not frighten me, though Hector's ears pricked up, and I could feel his anxiousness.

"Do not worry," I told him, my hand caressing his neck. "Old Bear has no intention of eating horse or boy. He is only just waking up and going about his business of being a bear."

When we came to the edge of town, I rode slowly down the main street, nodding to folk going about their business. For some reason, I did not want to ride up to Elizabeth's house, though I had done that often in the past. I was afraid that she would turn me away, would think that I had come to confront her again. It would be much better, I thought, if I could just happen upon her somewhere. But where might that be?

I knew of a small shop in the village where women shopped for lace and bolts of cloth. It was there that some folk gathered, and gossip was exchanged. Perhaps that would be a good place to find her—or at least, get some idea of where she might be. But no, I thought, folk would wonder. Men and boys did not often visit this shop.

The minister's house? It would be appropriate for Elizabeth to visit Abigail to see how she was feeling.

Perhaps I should go there and see for myself?

No, I was only fooling myself. Elizabeth would not visit Abigail, not unless things had changed much since last I saw her. But by then, with all my mulling things over back and forth, I found myself in the vicinity of the minister's house. Well, I decided to stop there and go on to Elizabeth's afterward, though a voice inside me whispered, "Coward".

I had come up by the road along the back of the house, and there, I dismounted and tied Hector to a post. My leg was hurting me from the long ride, and I stretched and flexed it, urging the muscles to loosen. When it felt a little better, I slowly made my way along the grassy path to the house, limping, perhaps even more than usual. As I came around the corner of the house, I heard voices—laughter. I looked and saw Abigail and several other girls sitting on the grass or perched on the stone wall surrounding the kitchen garden. They were Ann Putnam and Mercy Lewis and Mary Warren . . . Mary Warren! She was a maid. What was she doing with the girls?

Elizabeth? No, no Elizabeth.

The girls were laughing loudly, and I saw then that Ann had begun a performance. She stood up, staggered, her head whipping back and forth, her hands flailing wildly. She danced around in the grass

that way for a moment, twirling and shaking.

Was she possessed again? She was! She was being tormented. But then, she bent over laughing and fell onto the grass, her skirts outstretched. The others joined in the laughter.

"Wonderful! Perfect!" Mercy Lewis cried out, clapping her hands. "No one does it better. You seemed to have ten spirits possessing you."

"Nay, watch me. I can do even better!" Abigail said. She stood up. She moved to the circle of grass where Ann had just been. She held out her arms. She smiled.

And then, she looked up and saw me.

"George!" she cried, dropping her arms. "George Corwin!"

All of the girls turned to me at once.

For a moment, no one spoke, as we looked over each other. The girls seemed stunned. What were they thinking? What had they been doing?

After a moment of watching each other silently, Ann Putnam spoke. "The judge's son," she said softly. "Well. And what did you see, George? Did you see us at play?"

I did not answer.

"What do you think that you saw?" she asked again.

"I am not sure what I saw," I said slowly. And that was the truth. Had I witnessed a performance? Had they been rehearsing their actions for the courtroom?

Had they been pretending all along, as Elizabeth said that they were? I felt myself trembling inside. With fear? With anger?

"Well?" Ann said. "Speak up. Why did you come? And what did you see? What do you think you saw?"

"I came to see . . . I came to see how Abigail is feeling."

Abigail had moved closer to Ann. In fact, all of the girls had gathered close to each other. Both Abigail and Mary Warren looked pale. Ann, though, seemed like her usual self—cold, domineering, clearly the one in charge.

"Abigail is fine," she said. "Though she is pale, as you can see."

"Yes," I said. "I can see that. How be you, Abigail?"

Abigail looked at Ann. It seemed to me that she was pleading with her eyes. For what?

"Tell him," Ann said. "Tell him how you continue to be tormented. Tell him about the witch gathering and how you refused that evil red sacrament."

But Abigail did not tell me. She did not say a word. She simply shook her head and then sank down on the wall. Ann sat beside her. She took Abigail's hands in her own, rubbing them lightly. Then she looked up at me.

"Abigail is cold. Her hands are like ice. She is about to be taken over by demons again. Are you a

witch, George?" she asked.

Abigail shuddered and leaned against Ann.

"I think that you should leave quickly," Ann said to me. "And George? Do not forget this: boys have been accused. I do not think that you would like that to happen. Would you, George?"

Chapter Seven

The evil was back upon us, though most likely it had never left. It was simply that the spring had tricked me. The new court had now met, and the girls had made their accusations, and the witches were condemned.

My heart was in torment. Had the girls been performing that day? Had they been playing? Had they been practicing? I tried to tell Papa what I had seen, but he dismissed it. Of course, the girls would be talking about it among themselves, he said. Why would they not? It was a dreadful thing that was happening to them. Just about the only thing that made Papa pause was when I told him that the girls were laughing. He seemed to mull that over, but he said nothing more. And so, the day came when I went with Papa and an enormous crowd up Prison Lane, alongside the stone walls that lined the way to the pasture, and on up the hill. The weather had turned even milder, and the sun shone hot on our shoulders. The lane was dusty, and the few trees gave little shade.

It was a steep hill, and the wagon wheels groaned under their burden—and a fierce burden it was, for there were two carts, and in each cart were the witches. In one were Sarah Good and Sarah Wildes.

In the other were Susannah Martin, Elizabeth Howe—and Rebecca Nurse. All five were about to be hanged. A guard of horsemen accompanied us, raising dust so thick that it was hard to breathe at times.

I felt an intense sorrow in my heart over Rebecca Nurse, and, God help me, doubts that had plagued me for weeks now. Papa must have felt my doubts, though, except for that one time, I never said them aloud. But he had taken every opportunity to assure me that what we were doing was right. This very morning, he had said that although the punishment was severe, it was the only way to rid ourselves of the devil's plague.

With the new court of Oyer and Terminer, I also knew that there would be many more hangings. Everyone who had been brought in front of the court, no matter how she professed her innocence, was found guilty. Every. Single. One.

Strange, though—those who admitted to being a witch and rejected the devil were often set free. Today, the women who were about to be hanged had each proclaimed her innocence. And yet women like Tituba, who freely admitted to being witches, were happily allowed to live. I prayed that my concerns would not cause me to be distracted from what was right. I also dared not let Papa know how I felt, for he seemed at ease with what was

about to occur. He had even made me come along today because he believed that if our community had condemned these witches to death, we should see the result of our condemnation.

We were about halfway up the hill, when the carts suddenly halted and the horses balked. The first cart began to slip back down the little and toward the second cart, the horses scrabbling at the dirt with their hooves.

"'Tis the devil!" someone muttered.

"'Tis the horses!" answered Sheriff Walcott. "Get up there, you!" he yelled at the horses. They moved on just a little, then again hesitated, and again, the crowd began calling down shouts and curses upon the heads of the witches. Some of the condemned were wailing and praying aloud, some defiant and angry. It took a few moments of encouragement and even whipping of the horses, before we all moved on.

In the moment of pausing for the horses, I had focused on the face of Rebecca Nurse. Unlike the others in the cart, she seemed calm, even peaceful. How could that be? She was not angry. She was not defiant. She was—or seemed to be—at peace with her God.

The very appearance of her peaceful face caused my heart to thud heavily inside of me. Papa had

judged them. Papa had found them guilty. He and the others had condemned them to die. Now was not the time to doubt.

I clicked my tongue at Hector and moved up until I was abreast of Papa. Perhaps just being near his strength would raise strength in my own heart.

Papa turned to me. "Reverend Noyes will say the sermon this morning," he said. "Even now, some may repent and confess. We can only pray that they will go before their God in peace."

"Will they say the Lord's Prayer, Papa?"

"We shall see," Papa said. "The devil can surely work his evil even in these moments. We shall wait and see. Now take care to observe everything that happens here today. Remember it. You are a witness. We honor God as we remove these witches from our midst. This is how we revere our God."

I nodded and swallowed hard. I looked at the trees, the empty nooses swinging silently from them, moving slightly in the breeze. The women waited somberly or angrily. The crowd awaited their death.

This is how we revere our God. I whispered it to myself. *This is how we revere our God.*

Papa leaned in close to me and put a hand on my arm. I knew then that he was aware of my doubts. I could not look at him. Something was happening inside of me, doubts were coming into full bloom.

But so late. Oh, it was so late. We rode on side by side and reined in our horses near the gallows trees.

The first to be taken down from the cart was Sarah Good. I watched as ropes were wound around her skirts, tying her legs together at the ankles. Her hands were tied behind her back. The crowd, that had been noisy and chaotic, became hushed then, in the moment before the hood was placed over her head.

"The last judgment is near, Sarah Good," Reverend Noyes said. "Confess now! You are a witch, and you know that you are a witch. Even now, in Christ's mercy, now in the shadow of the noose, there is time for repentance. Confess before you go before your God."

Sarah Good pulled herself up as best as she could, tied up in the way that she was. Her face, however, showed no repentance at all. It was hard and cold.

"You are a liar!" she said, and though she was standing down on the ground, out of sight of the people in the back of the crowd, she spoke loudly enough that I was sure everyone could hear. "I," she said, "am no more a witch than you are a wizard!"

I turned to Papa. Even he looked surprised. At the foot of the gallows, how could any person not repent? At every public hanging—every single one—the accused always repented. One must. One

was on one's way to judgment. Was this perhaps the sign—the sign that I needed—that she was indeed a witch?

"Do you not repent?" Reverend Noyes responded. "How can you not repent before your God? Have you no more to say? No repentance, no words to God to offer before the noose takes away your life?"

"Yes, I have words to say!" Sarah Good exclaimed. "I say this." Her voice dropped away, and for a moment, there was utter silence. When she looked up again, she spoke loudly. "I say this: if you take away my life, God will give you blood to drink!"

I felt a shudder run through my body, a shudder as though I had been cursed. Muttering rose up from the crowd. Then, Sheriff Walcott dropped the hood over her head. He tied it tightly around her neck. He slung her over his shoulder as though she was no more than a bag of grain. She did not struggle. She could not struggle. He carried her to the ladder that stood beside the tree, where the noose hung empty, swinging in the slight breeze. Four more nooses hung from four more trees.

There was complete silence in the crowd. Shadows of clouds had moved across the sun all morning, but as Sheriff Walcott climbed the ladder,

with Sarah Good slung over his shoulder, the sun burst out hot and strong. A finch called from a nearby tree. It was answered by another.

The noose was dropped over Sarah Good's head.

In a moment, Sheriff Walcott would climb down. The ladder would be kicked out from under her. And Sarah Good would swing, her neck broken, her soul rising up to God. And to judgment.

I turned away.

There was a sound. The fall of the ladder. A thud. The creaking of the rope. A sigh went up from the crowd. I had not looked, but I knew that it had happened. I turned back but averted my eyes from what hung from the tree.

I looked around the crowd, wondering if Elizabeth was among us. I did not see her, though I thought that I saw her papa at the edge of the crowd.

I turned back to the next accused—to Rebecca Nurse. As the sheriff prepared her, tying her arms, then tying her skirts and her legs together, Reverend Parris moved close to Papa and me. He nodded at me, but from the way that he moved his horse between us, it was clear that he wanted to speak to Papa privately. I reined Hector back a little to be proper. But still, I listened closely. I heard some words: "It is a sad business." And then I heard the word, "friends."

58

Papa replied, "Even so." And he nodded.

My heart began thudding so hard that I thought for sure it could be heard all the way to the gallows. Was Reverend Parris suggesting that one of Papa's friends was to be accused next? Is that what those words meant? Someone in Elizabeth's family, perhaps, Papa's oldest and dearest friend? Or did it mean something else completely?

I looked at Papa, but his face was just calm and thoughtful, and I thought that it could not have been what I feared. After all, Papa had many friends, not just Elizabeth's family. And maybe they were only talking business—money, something like that?

Reverend Parris moved away, again nodding to me, then made his way to the front of the throng where they had prepared Rebecca Nurse for the gallows.

While she was bound, but before the hood was thrown over her head, she too was given a chance to repent and confess.

She spoke softly but clearly, and in contrast to the way that Sarah Good had spoken. Her voice was calm, sweet even. "The Lord knows," she said. "The Lord alone, who is the searcher of hearts, knows that as I shall answer it at the tribunal seat, as I will shortly appear, that I know not the least thing of witchcraft. Therefore, I cannot, I durst not, belie my own soul."

At that moment, the hood was thrown over her head, and she was carried, as Sarah Good had been before her, like a sack up the ladder to where the noose hung.

I turned away, as I did before. I did not, could not, look upon what was about to happen. And as I looked around, I knew that I was not alone in the crowd with my doubts. Many faces looked drawn, troubled, and not, I felt sure, by the simple fact of death. I believe that many of us harbored doubts, thoughts that perhaps innocent people were going to their deaths. And those of us who sent them there were guilty.

Three more women were hanged that morning. And while I longed to run away from that place, I forced myself to stay. My heart had grown thick and heavy in my chest, and my throat ached. Was it in sympathy with those whose necks were strung out there before me? Five bodies now hung limp, legs wrapped, heads bowed. Necks broken.

And inside me, the word "friend" whispered around in my mind. *Friend. It is a sad business.*

It was a solemn crowd that turned toward home. And solemn I was, also. I resolved that if it was Elizabeth or her family who was accused, they were not going to hang. Accused, perhaps, for

I could not stop that. But escape, they could. I would do everything in my power to make that happen.

For Elizabeth was no more a witch than I was a wizard.

Chapter Eight

Papa was silent on our way back to the village that afternoon. He said that we would not be leaving the village to return home that evening as we had planned. Instead, we would stay at Ingersoll's Tavern for one more day, as he had business to attend to. He did not explain what the business was, but I feared that I knew—especially since he would not tell me directly.

And if it was what I suspected, what should I do? Warn her. But how? I knew that she visited the child, Dorcas Good, in the jail. Should I go there tonight and wait for her? But then, would I be accused for being in her company? And was I not betraying Papa by doing so?

Was I betraying my own soul by doing so? Or by not doing so?

When we arrived at the tavern and had stabled our horses, Papa and I went to the main room for a glass of cider and rum. The room was noisy with revelers, as though it was a holiday—the kind of day to rejoice in the harvest or in good planting. I could hardly believe the atmosphere. We had just put five women to death!

"Papa?" I said, when we were settled at a table in a far corner, as faraway as we could be from the

throng of men who had already congregated there. "Papa, what think you?"

I did not dare ask what I wanted to ask: do you still believe that those women are witches? Are you really going to accuse Elizabeth or her mama or her papa, your dear friends?

For a long time, Papa did not answer. He merely stared down into his glass of rum, marking rings on the table with the moisture from the glass. I kept my eyes on him, waiting. His face was drawn and tired, and I noted that dark rings had appeared under his eyes. His shoulders drooped, and for a moment, I thought: *why, he is old!* My papa had never appeared old to me before. I wondered how much this weighed on his conscience, what he had been doing.

After a very long time, he looked up at me. "What do I think, George? I think that God just may have abandoned our village. I wonder, George. I do wonder."

I sucked in my breath. Papa is truly religious—the most prayerful, godly man I know. How grieved he must be to say such a thing! I waited a long moment, hoping, praying, that he would voice a doubt. For if he did, I could confide in him. Perhaps even—would I dare ask him to help me save Elizabeth?

"What is it you wonder, Papa?" I asked finally.

Papa looked up at me, and his eyes had that pale,

watery look that I have only seen in old men. "I wonder, George, if Reverend Parris is correct. He says that sinners and wicked people can hide in the covenant of the church. He says that God allows the devil to tempt." He paused.

"Yes, Papa?" I said, prompting him.

"He also preaches that God will not allow the devil to take over the bodies of truly holy people," he went on. "But I believe that He has allowed it. I do believe that He has. Rebecca Nurse, one of the church's holiest women, yet she went to her death unrepentant."

I dropped my eyes.

"It makes my heart quake inside of me," Papa went on. "Who can one trust? Who is truly part of God's covenant? I am afraid to look at times. I am afraid that there is so much more to come. I am afraid the Last Judgment is near. Perhaps even the devil is afraid, for he knows that he too will be judged."

I nodded, but I could not look into Papa's face. I had hoped so much that he would express a doubt. How could he not? I now knew for sure that I could not ask for his help. But more than that, what was wrong with me that what I saw was so different from what Papa saw? I had witnessed the same events, but I saw them all so differently.

Yet Papa was older and wiser than I was. He was

a judge. He was a church elder. He prayed constantly.

Surely I was the sinner who should repent.

Papa looked up and around the room. The noise had become so loud that it was becoming harder and harder to be heard, as men had more and more to drink.

One man standing at the bar caught Papa's eye and saluted him with a glass raised up high. Several other men then turned to us, stood up, and saluted us.

"We hanged five hell witches!" exclaimed one, and he raised his glass to Papa.

"Impudent witches!" another shouted. "Even when the noose hung above their heads!"

Papa stood then and motioned for me to do so also. "Take your book to the front room by the fire," he said. "There is far too much uproar here."

I stood up and moved toward the front room, but Papa did not follow me. Instead, he crossed the room to the bar, and I wondered what he would say to those men. Would he agree with them? Would he scold them for harboring such thoughts when so serious a matter was consuming us? I did not know, but I was glad to escape from that place.

In the front room, I found myself a seat by the fire. It was hardly a quiet room, though, and in a few moments, more men—a few of them drunk on rum—settled there also. Perhaps it is because I am

only a boy. Perhaps it was because of the alcohol. But they spoke in front of me as though I was not there.

"Another witch—and that a child!" cried a red-bearded man whom I recognized as Nathaniel Harper, a carpenter who sometimes worked for Papa. He settled himself at the table right beside my chair and winked at me. "These girls have been assaulted by so many witches, one cannot follow," he said. "What think you, young man? You are not a witch, are ye?"

At that, my heart jumped up into my throat. To be accused that way was dangerous, was . . .

But Nathaniel just slapped my thigh, laughing. He turned back to his friend. "No witch, this young man. But do ye believe, Charlie, sixty-five witches to date have attacked Ann Putnam. Sixty-five! There's plenty more to hang now."

"Aye," said the man that he had called Charlie, a dark-bearded, swarthy man—a farmer by the look of his cheeks and hardened hands. "We will string up every one of 'em. Unrepentant witches!"

"Ah, and that Sarah Good, calling down blood on the sheriff. And now, another child has been named." The farmer turned to me. "Ye are knowing her, are ye not? That Elizabeth Putnam?"

My heart drummed frantically in my chest, and I felt my cheeks burn. Should I go to the jail? Or was

it too late in the evening for her to be there? The other evening, it had been just barely dark when she went there. Now, darkness had fallen fully, and the moon was beginning to stream in the corners of the tavern windows.

I held my breath for a moment, then nodded. "Yes, sir," I said, and I trembled inside, not just for Elizabeth, but for myself. One could not even be associated with witches—accused witches. "Our fathers are . . ." Did I dare say it? "Are . . . friends."

"And your papa will set her straight!" he said. "Convict and hang her, right my man?"

I nodded and hoped that by the dim candlelight, he could not see what must have been on my face.

"Her father is too proud with his carriages and servants. And his daughter all decked out in lace and ribbons," said Nathaniel. "She will see what good her father's gold does her in jail."

"The rats will eat her pretty ribbons!" Charlie replied. And then both men burst into drunken laughter.

They ordered more ale then, and I went back to my reading—or pretending to read—as thoughts swirled in my head. What should I do? What could I do?

"Ah, but I know something," Nathaniel said, leaning in close to his friend and looking at me, too.

"Her papa is a clever one. I hear that he keeps his horses saddled up, ready to go." He put his hand on my thigh again. "Tell your papa about this. He may not know. He will not want them to escape the noose, will he, now?"

"Keeps his horses saddled, does he?" said Charlie, grinning at Nathaniel. "I have heard that also. Perhaps tomorrow—no, even this night—we can take care of them."

Nathaniel let out a whoop of laughter and leaned back in his chair. "Maybe even start a little fire?"

"Oh, no, friend, not that," the farmer said. "Too easy for it to spread. My farm is not far away. But something. Eh, Nathaniel?"

Nathaniel nodded and took a swig of his ale. "I helped cut them down," he said.

"Buried them?" Charlie asked.

"Right there in the field."

"Took their hoods off?" Charlie asked.

"That I did," said Nathaniel.

"What did they look like dead?"

I stood up. I did not want to hear what they looked like dead. I tried not to draw too much attention to myself and eased myself away from the fire.

But I was not quick enough, because behind me, I heard, "Their tongues stick out! Ever seen a

witch's tongue?"

There was a lot of laughter then, as though all of the men in the room were suddenly a part of what had been a small, private conversation.

"Black!" Nathaniel shouted. "Witches' tongues are black."

I fled the room and the tavern. My bad leg ached from the long day, from the long ride out to the hangings and back. But it did not matter. I had to go to Elizabeth, and if it was wrong, I could only pray that God would forgive me someday. But I had one mission now and one only: to save Elizabeth's life, to protect her from my very own father.

Chapter Nine

Was it wrong, what I was about to do? Was it right? Would God ever forgive me? And if my papa found out, would *he* ever forgive me? My thoughts ran around in my head like little mice in a barrel of oats. Do it. Do not do it. Go there, warn her. Do not go, she will not speak to you anyway.

Then tell her papa. But, no, he was furious at my papa and might think that it was all a trick. Papa had refused to allow little Dorcas to be freed, and I know that it infuriated Elizabeth's papa. They had had a terrible quarrel over it. When Elizabeth's papa had left the tavern that night, he had been furious. I had come in just as he was leaving and heard him accuse Papa of being thick-headed and stupid. Not many people call Papa stupid, and those who do surely pay a price. The two of them had not spoken since. So why would he believe me? If he would even agree to speak with me?

There was only one thing that I could think of to do, and it was this: stand guard over the barn by myself. Find a hidden spot, and if I saw anyone approach, I could see what they were up to. If I could do nothing else, I could cry out. The shout of "Fire!" never fails to bring men running.

But before I went there, I had to provide myself with a warm cloak and some food. Even though the

night was heavy and hot, I knew that by dawn, dampness would begin to make my leg throb. Wrapping myself up in a cloak would help with the pain, and some cheese and bread could ward off sleep.

I went up to my room, took a sack, and into it I stuffed my cloak and my sketchbook. Then, I went down to the bar room. There, I found myself some bread and cheese and some hard-cooked eggs. The men were still drinking and laughing, and no one seemed to pay me any attention. I tucked the food into my sack.

Once again, I slipped out and into the still night.

Night creatures were making a racket in the grass, and others chirped from up above me in the trees. There was a seesawing sound all around me, as though the night was alive with songs. A bird called, and I thought how strange and joyful it has always seemed to me to hear bird calls at night. This night, though, there was no joy in pondering such things.

I made my way across the field, the thick night air heavy around me. In the distance, I could see Elizabeth's house, candles lit in the windows downstairs, the upstairs darkened. I wondered if she and her parents were talking about the affairs of the day, thinking about the hangings. Elizabeth must have felt devastated by the death of Rebecca Nurse, and I did also. She was a woman of God.

71

She even went to her death as a woman of God. And as we had put her to death, would God forgive us?

My head throbbed and ached almost as much as my leg did. Weeds and knee-high grasses grabbed at my pant legs, and once, I stepped in a hole and stumbled. It was only a ten-minute walk and then the house was right in front of me. I made a wide circle around it so that I would not be seen. The barn loomed up behind the house a fair distance, approached by a long lane. I did not walk on the pebbled lane for fear of making a sound, but instead I stuck to the grasses along the edge. When I reached the barn, I noticed that the doors were open, and, yes—several horses were saddled! So they knew, they did know. They knew that they were about to be accused. They were clever to be ready to flee. And yet, they must have known that if they were accused—even if they fled—all of their possessions would be claimed by the judges and turned over to the courts.

I wondered how long they had known that they were under suspicion? Did they have a story prepared for their inquisitors? It needed to be a good one, but even so, words were twisted horribly in court. I had seen that myself. Goodwife Nurse had said that accused witches were, "of our company." She begged

and explained later that she did not mean that they were *witches* with her. She explained that she merely meant that they were *prisoners* with her. The court— my papa—refused to accept her explanation and used her very own words against her.

I walked quietly around the back of the barn, looking for a place to hide myself, yet a place where I could see what I needed to see. There was a small lean-to type structure on one side of the barn, with a small ledge where saws and farm implements were stored and hung. I could sit on the ledge or, perhaps, hide myself underneath it, if need be.

I had just come around the side of the barn, when I saw the door to the back of the house open and someone step out. I quickly stepped back into the shadow of the barn. But I did not need to worry. It was simply the maid, come to dump a pail of water out into the yard. She stayed there for a moment, looking around her, as I held as still as death. She sank down on the back step, wiping her face in her apron. She was new to our town—an Irish girl from Boston—and I wondered what she thought about the madness that had afflicted us. After a few moments, she raised herself up and returned to the house, and I breathed easily again.

I made my way back to the lean-to and settled myself for a long wait. The night became darker,

and the candles on the first floor of the house were snuffed out. I watched as candlelight flickered in the upper rooms and then the whole house was still and dark and silent as the grave.

I do not know how long I watched—hours, perhaps. And then, in that darkest part of the night, just before dawn, I heard something. It was a sound from inside the barn, the sound of men moving around, muttered sounds.

My heart leaped into my throat. I had not heard nor seen them coming. Oh, no, what was wrong with me? Why had I allowed myself to sleep?

I was just pulling myself up when I saw the figures—two figures—leave the barn, crouched, making their way silently into the field. As soon as they were gone, I leaped off the ledge and ran on tiptoe into the barn.

All appeared well. The horses were still there. They were still saddled. I sniffed the air. There was no odor of fire. What had happened? What had they done? Cautiously, I made my way around the barn, looking in the stalls, moving slowly and silently. The horses noticed my presence and snorted; one of them stomping and whinnying lightly.

"Quiet, quiet!" I spoke softly to him, then once again made my way around the barn, peering into every corner. Nothing seemed harmed, nothing

seemed out of place.

What, then? Surely they had not been here for no reason.

I moved to the saddled horses and ran my hands over their flanks. "Everything is fine," I soothed them. "All is good."

I felt for their harnesses and saddles. And then I had a thought. I felt under their stomachs and found it. I found the trick that the men had been up to. All three horses were saddled. All three saddles were fine. But underneath, on the belly of the horse, things were not fine at all. The cinches had been loosened. And on one horse, the cinch had been cut. When Elizabeth and her parents leaped onto the horses to escape, they would not notice that anything was wrong. Until they began to gallop away—when the saddles would slip and turn. They would either fall from their horses, or the horses would falter and stop. Either way, pursuers would find them and bring them back.

Quickly, I went to work. I tightened the cinch on each of the two horses, testing them again and again to be sure that they would not slip. Then I looked around me. There was no way that I could repair the cut cinch. Surely, there must be another saddle. I hurried to the back of the barn. Daylight was beginning to break over the horizon, and I

could hear birds calling now. Soon, I would no longer be working under the cover of darkness, and I had to hurry.

In the saddle room at the back of the barn, I found several saddles hanging on the wall. I chose one that seemed heavy and sturdy enough and brought it back to where the saddled horses stood.

Then, still moving as swiftly and silently as I was able, I removed the saddle with the cut cinch and resaddled the horse. I tightened the cinch, then looked around me. Surely, Elizabeth's papa would notice that a saddle had been changed. But perhaps he would think that it had been done by a servant. At any rate, he would be—they all would be—safe. Or as safe as anyone could be in this madness that was now Salem.

Chapter Ten

It *was* Elizabeth who was accused. I heard about it from my papa, who had sent men to the house that evening to address her and her mama and papa. And then, that night, they made their escape from this terrible town. They escaped, and more, they took the child Dorcas with them, though how Elizabeth managed that, I did not know for the longest time. All I knew that summer was that terror and horror haunted our village and our town.

The court of Oyer and Terminer was convened to find guilt and punish the witches. The summer dragged on, with more and more accusations and more hangings. Finally, in September, something even more awful and terrible happened, something that made folk stop. And think. Giles Corey, an old man— a very old man—was accused. He refused to even allow himself to be brought to court. He said that it was a sham. He refused to speak in his own defense. And so, he was pressed to death by stones. It was the verdict of the court that it must be done—the verdict of my papa. It was done in the center of the village. They bound him and lay him on a board. They heaped stones and rocks upon him and then more stones, and still he would not speak, would not even defend himself. They continued to pile on the stones. It took

two days for him to die. And in those two days, I fled Salem.

I left my papa behind and fled. I left everything—perhaps even my senses. I only had Hector, my horse, my sketchbook, and what was left of my soul. I never returned to that town. I never returned to my parents' home. For how could I live with my papa and what he had done? Surely, he did what he believed that he must do. But was that a reason to be excused? Was he ever to be forgiven? By God? By me? There were too many questions for me, and so I fled. We had family in Boston, and I knew that they would take me in for a while, until I found a trade or some work to support me. Perhaps I would go out on a sailing vessel, for at sea, my bad leg would not be much of a hindrance.

It was while I was on the dock in Boston one day that following winter that I met Elizabeth. She had come to the dock where her papa's ships were berthed, bringing him a message. I was there looking for work; I needed to get away, and the sea held great appeal.

For a moment, I know that Elizabeth did not recognize me. I had put on some weight and knew that I was looking more like a man. But she, she was still the beautiful young girl I had always loved.

"Elizabeth?" I said, as she hurried by me.

She turned, her face questioning. "George?" she said. "George Corwin, is that you?"

"It is," I replied.

Neither of us spoke then, and I know not what spun around in her head, but in mine was only sadness and a memory of the last time that we spoke—and the anger with which she had accused me.

"How be you?" she asked finally, her voice cold.

"Well enough," I answered. "And you?"

"We are recovering," she said. "Dorcas is well."

I smiled. "I am glad." And then, maybe because of my guilt, maybe something else, maybe just a need to make things well with her, I do not know. But I had to tell her.

"I kept watch over you that last night, you know," I said. "I kept your horses safe from the drunkards."

She frowned at me. "You did what?"

"They had loosened the cinches. I fixed them."

Still, she frowned at me. "Did you saddle up one horse? With an old saddle?"

I nodded. "They had cut that cinch. I could not repair it."

She put a hand to her chest. "So that is what happened! Papa has wondered for the longest time. You did that?"

I nodded.

"*You* did that?" she said again. "You did not betray us?"

"I tried to save you," I replied.

And then, she did something that no girl does—no girl in Salem, anyway. But we were in Boston now, and perhaps things were more free. More honest, at least. She threw her arms around my neck and hugged me.

"It is over, George," she whispered, looking up at me, tears welling up in her eyes.

I nodded. "It is over," I answered back, but my voice choked in my throat.

Because it was not really over. It had only ended. It would linger forever with both of us, with all of us. But it had ended. Thank God, it had ended.